The Mirror He Shattered

Emmett Barber

Contents

Chapter 1

Flashes of light and voices called out to the man, all attention focused on him at this moment as he simply kept his gaze forward and walked down the hall, making sure to hold onto the hand in his own hand. The weight of the hand in his, even though it was a small hand, was heavier than imagined, reminding him of the oath he had taken when he became a parent. He looked down to the child, offering her a warm smile, wanting her to feel comfortable as she experienced a new type of evening tonight, one of cameras and a commotion of people calling out to him. The woman beside him was one of beauty to be envied, her lips planting a soft kiss on his cheek as they ascended the marble stairs.

As he picked up the child and rested her on his hip, the woman beside him reminded him of what tonight would bring, how it would end, and how the new world would begin. They both knew that the future he was going to bring upon himself would contort their once fairytale life. They both knew the reality that they would face tomorrow, one which even they were unsure of as fear only laced its way through their hearts and scared them. As a child, he was raised to be the best he could and learned how he adorned the idea of shocking others. He realized how to articulate his very career into one of shocking the public, for they wanted entertained, perhaps that form not even science could explain. Having taken the public's desires and molding them with his hobby, he crafted it not only into his career, but into his life as well.

The woman beside him took his hand in hers, her silk gloves causing him to recall the texture of her hair that was pinned back tonight in effortless curls, those black locks mimicking gentle waves. A pair of piercing green eyes, they look towards the entrance of the performance hall, her hand squeezing his tight for reassurance as she knew that tonight had to happen, but she was still unsure how she could go along with her future. She knew of the troubles which would arise within an hour, for it was not just her husband who knew how to work the crowd, but this woman as well, for she was the one who stood by his side every night...who would stand by his side one last night.

Security guards opened a set of doors for the family as they took a turn, the hallway stretched long before them as the doors closed behind them. Not another soul was within the hallway, causing the reporters outside to seem as if they lived in another world, the commotion outside only muffled as the family walked further away from the doors.

Tonight would be a full house, even the president in the audience with a few other world leaders and individuals held in high regard to the public eye. After all, this man was one of the most successful in his field, for he knew how to captivate an audience. His name was internationally famous for even his younger days as a university student traveling the globe he had even preformed for the royalty of Middle Eastern and Asian countries, leading to his fame in the Western world with more world leaders in favor of his performances. The presence of these types of people here tonight did not frighten him tonight, for it was where he would be once the show ended that he was afraid of.

As the family entered into the room, the man set his daughter down on the couch, looking to his wife as she adjusted her diamond jewelry and pushed back a few stray hairs. It was a habit of his wife to do this as a way to calm her nerves, to just stand before a mirror and adjust things to perfection as she would allow herself to calm down. The couple both looked to their daughter for a short second as she kicked off her shoes and closed her eyes. The very definition of innocence within a world of sin. Their daughter had no idea what tonight would bring for the family, for she had no idea she would never see her father again. Her father would be mothering but a memory in just an hour.

The man kissed his wife's temple, whispering words to her as she turned to him, wanting to plead with him to rethink his plans tonight. She could not imagine living a life without him, but she knew that no matter it would break her heart, she had always known this night would come and that this was that night. Her husband had analyzed the ancient writings and legends before applying his knowledge as part of his career and unlike most of the world, he did not believe magic was just a word for something you could not comprehend. Traveling the world for years with only his passport, a backpack, and enough money for a meal, he learned his way around, learned languages thought to be dead, and spells to be merely childish words.

Tonight would be his life's last work here in this world and it was not just some silly prop, but something he had spent many years perfecting. This trick was not just pure magic, but something so real that it would tamper with the fabric of reality.

He had never used it to its full potential, he had never dared try it like he would tonight, but as the minutes passed by and his time with his family grew thin, he knew that the path before him could end in various ways. His wife granted him one last kiss as he reached into his pocket, pulling out a key as he handed it over to his wife. Looking over to his daughter, he whispered the instructions to his wife as she took the key. His daughter would never understand what this item meant to him, why he had to leave it, and why he had to preform the trick which he did tonight, for she would grow up believing her father died in a tragic accident and he was lifeless before help could arrive.

His daughter would grow up believing her father never completed his life's world and that the family name would only hold the value of tragedy after this night. As a man called from the other side of the door that it was time, the wife put on her best smile and her husband took her hand as they said goodbye to their daughter.

As they walked to the back of the stage, he saw on the stage the very object which he would use to take him to another world. The lights blinded the couple as they walked onto the stage, the crowd rising to their feet as they cheered for the man and his wife. As he introduced themselves and the show for the night, his wife walked to the prop, pulling away the black fabric as the crowd fell silent in awe. The simple mirror with engravings of an ancient cult from ancient times in the Middle East, the mirror had a simple look to it, nothing more than what a prop would look like to the average eye.

As the man stepped up to create the final act of his life, he saw, from the corner of his eyes, his daughter, smiling and waving as her father vanished into the mirror...into a realm she would soon enter into as well.

Chapter 2

It calls to me, every day, the same door that I've told myself to never walk past. Sure, I've been in there countless of times, often entering when I think of my father, just sitting on his chair as I look at myself in that mirror, the mirror that took him from me. Sometimes I think my parents never wanted me to see the show that night, that they never wanted to watch his final trick. I call it a freak accident. People call it a horrible happening to one of the greatest magicians to ever live. My mother calls it a tragedy and forever feels guilty. It resembles pain. It resembles the loss of the man she loved, the loss of her husband, and the loss of her only child's father.

But every magician has that one trick that they know will threaten them, at least the greatest do. My father was one of the greats, no one yet pushing the limits he broke. His final trick was a wake up call to all the other magicians, one that made them only more realize the ricks that they all take. Perhaps to the world of magic, they take my father's story as one of a great magic who let his arrogance get to him and destroy the very name he had built for himself.

"Candice!"

Turning around, I find my mother in the doorway, home from a day of work. Her job was once to join my father on stage as she assisted him. Their story was one many loved to hear, how the magician fell for his assistant. After my father died so many years ago, my mother went back to college, gaining even a doctorate where she specialized in string theory from Massachusetts Institute of Technology. Sometimes I think she chose that major because of my father, because of what he did. Father was smarter than many, physics was something he would study and implement into his tricks, applying insane theories that he had learned from the future professors of my mother. Mother never cleaned up his desk, all the notes he left behind with different equations and intense mathematical projections all in black ink. Yet academia was not all he used, for there were sketches of unusual symbols that mother tried to get rid of.

My father never saw his biggest trick complete. I don't know where he went. Many said my father had tried to make a portal, others said it was some trick with the reflection of mirrors and he was just hiding from us. But I believe what my mother says, how my father is gone from this world. I know she means the afterlife, that he is gone.

Every Christmas my grandmother tells me how proud he would be of me, how he is looking down from the heavens and smiling at me. She tells me if my father was here, he would be smiling and telling me how well I have turned out to be.

"Yes?" I ask, hopping off my father's desk where he once planned out his final trick. My mother told me he planned on retiring from the field of magic after that show. At school people either tell me how sorry they are that I lost my father at such a young age, or I hear the gossip of how he was a failure. A few come to me, talking of my father with high regards as they too hope to be just as great as he was. Father helped make magic something more than just a performance on some talent show, but a world-wide sensation.

My father made magic become something so many wanted to see, something even more popular than what it had ever been.

When he was searching the world as he learned magic, he would do tricks to gain money just for a meal, he would do tricks for a ride. After a while the royalty from different countries would come to him, wanting to see his tricks. Soon, after ten years of searching the world, he married my mother and as four years passed, they had me, and their talents were known throughout the world.

"I know this is very sudden, Candice," my mother begins, but I already know what she will say. "I just booked a flight to Iceland for tomorrow." She does this very often. No, not for leisure, but for study. I know my mother is searching to understand my father's final trick, to try and see what happened to him.

"When will you come back?"

I ask that question every time, never giving up hope that she knows when she will be back, but she never knows. She once left me for three months when I was ten to be cared for by her best friend. I guess now she can afford to be gone longer than that, just because I recently graduated high school. Within seven weeks I'll be gone for college, allowing my mother the freedom to be gone and live to her own schedule. But that has never stopped her before. She's missed more than half of my birthdays, five Christmases, almost all my Thanksgivings, and even my graduation. But I still love her. She is still the woman that raised me in the absence of my father.

"I want to be home by next Wednesday," she replies. Six days to be gone. I have an equation that I use for her time estimates: take the number and multiple it by three. If she doesn't give you a day or date, that means she could be gone from two days to four months. "And then we will go and do some dorm shopping."

I already know I'll have to do all of that on my own. I even booked a flight to visit my college without her. She didn't come to scholarship night at the college when I got a small trophy for my full ride scholarship, she didn't even open the text of my prom dress when I sent her it.

I only know what it feels like to be alone, like a piece of my father that my mother tries to forget just as she sometimes tries to forget him. When he left to wherever he went, he took a piece of her with him, never to return it.

And I know she feels the same.

I know she loves me, but she loved and still loves my father. She is still searching for answers eleven years later. She is so determined that she has become an absent mom. Every week when she's gone I get a check in the mail for the weeks grocery money and that's about it. When I told her I was off to work one day, she had no idea that I had been working at a local business for several months.

"Okay," I reply, offering her a warm smile. "I'll look forward to it."

I already know she won't be there when I move into my dorm. But I know she's taught me one thing for sure, she's taught me to always be there for my family. She's taught me through her poor examples. Through her prime example of motherly qualities, I know the exact type of woman I want to become if I have children. Sure, no one is perfect when it comes to raising a family, but when you make no effort after your husband dies, it is selfish to not get over the past and try to do your best for your family. But she is family, even after all she has done, she is family and I still love her.

Mom goes off, leaving me alone to my thoughts in my father's office as she shuts the door. Once again, the darkness surrounds me as I look at that mirror. For so long I've wanted to see how it worked, how to operate the thing. Sometimes I daydream about to stepping into it and going wherever it takes me. Father's journal says it was to become a portal, but the only place it landed him was his grave. I've read through my father's journal time after time, the old book looking like Dr. Frankenstein's with all the sketches and graphs. My father was smart, a drop-out from Harvard who just wanted to see the world. He had gotten bored of studying for pre-law and wanted to show the world his tricks.

Sometimes I think there's some chant to operate this thing, other times I think it's a simple work of tools like a key or something.

Getting up, I walk towards the mirror once again. There a certain area that I always inspect, one with a small hole placed on the center of the frame, surrounded by a small engraving of letters that look ancient. Whatever this is, I deduced long ago that it was some part of importance. Leaning my head against the mirror, I stare at a reflection of myself, the dark brown locks that hit my mid-back, a set of dull brown eyes, fair skin, and the image of a girl who has never known what family truly feel like. I know that when my father was still around, that my mother and him tried to be there for everything I did. From every ballet recital to every small T-ball game I did.

Closing my eyes, I let out a deep breath, pushing off the mirror as I take in the rest of the office. Just as father left it, his desk covered in just his journal and two old pens from college, the curtains shut from the massive window, and items he used in performances covered in sheets. My dad worked years on this mirror, letting the others gain dusk. I remember fractions of my childhood when he was around, how he would work through the night to spend time with me during the day, how he always smiled when he saw me. It's been so long that I only remember what he looks like through pictures, but that smile he had, I shall always remember that part of him.

As I take a seat back on the chair, I open his journal. Looking at the pages as I flip them quickly, just as I flip the last page, I raise an eyebrow.

That's new. A small envelope, one with silver ink upon the opening, one of the ancient writing my father would study. Frantically I open the envelope, finding it to be a bit heavier than a letter from someone. Tearing apart the envelope, I only raise an eyebrow as a brass and rusting key falls onto my lap.

What? How did this get here?

Mom was just in this journal this morning, copying down some pictures onto her own journal. She said she was going to take the journal with her. Taking the key, I walk up to the mirror, looking at the hole. I push the key at the hole, only for it to be jammed midway. Nope, not the key. Hell, anybody could see this is not the key. This one looks like a house key while the hole in the mirror is circular. Way to go Candice.

Sighing, I shove the key into my pocket, looking back to the envelope. Something is important about this key though, how mom had it isolated in an envelope in dad's journal. She needs this or something like that.

That's when I decide to do something I'll never know if will harm my mother's journey tomorrow. Taking from one of my dad's drawers, an old key to his closet, grabbing an envelope as I place it in. Looking back at the original envelope, I take the same silver own from dad's desk, copying the ancient design correctly. The pluses of being an art student and even wanting to major in it. Then again, it could just be simple shape recognition a seven-year-old could match.

Placing the other envelope back in the journal, I keep the real key in my pocket, looking around. I've searched this office from head to toe, and I know there is no secret keyhole at all. Believe me, I've searched countless times. The only things in this house with keyholes are the doors, one massive chest in the living room for blankets, and mom's jewelry box that dad gave her.

That's it. That's got to be it! I run out of the room as my heart rate picks up quickly as I head up the stairs and into the massive master bedroom. How we were able to keep my childhood house still surprises me, but dad made quite the income with his job. Hell, the house was custom made just because of his work.

I hear mom downstairs, watching something on Netflix. Opening her room door, I find the modern yet homey room clean. There's one luggage by her bed, stuffed full of clothes you'd see on a dinosaur dig in the movies from the hat to boots. What is she digging for? I have no clue. I know dad did much of his beginning research in Iceland and she is following his every step.

Heading to the dresser in her huge closet, I find the jewelry box, handmade from Thailand, and with roses painted on the sides. The keyhole is slim, right in the middle. Grabbing the box, I recall all the times mom has opened it. I've never seen what it inside, but I remember her pulling out so many jewelry items from rubies to diamonds, from bronze to platinum.

As I take the key out, I take in a deep breath, hoping this works. Geronimo, it does work indeed, the key sliding in easily as I let out a deep breath.

Inside are multiple pieces of expensive jewelry my father gave her every chance he had to celebrate something. My eyes move across every piece, and that's when I see it, a necklace, one with a silver cylinder on the end. This would fit right into the hole. I take the necklace, closing her jewelry box, and dash out of the room. Running down the wooden stairs, I take a sharp left and head right back into the office.

Securing the door behind me, I can hear my mother calling my name. I must see if this will work.

My hands begin to shake as my mother knocks on the door, asking what is going on. Taking out the key, my fingers scuffle to get a decent grip on the key as they shake. Just as I hold it up to the hole, I shut my eyes, trying to calm down.

"Candice!"

I push it through, hearing it lock. It worked.

Opening my eyes, I see the mirror, but it's different this time. This time my reflection is different, this time my skin is black and my hair white. What the...

I look at my own body, at my skin, the light color, my brown locks. Is this just an effect of the mirror? It must be.

Reaching out to touch my reflection, I only gasp as my finger goes through.

"Candice, leave that damn mirror alone, don't you dare do any-thing!" Mom shouts, kicking and banging at the door. Dad made the door strong for a reason, dad made sure no one who threatened him could easily get in. "You have no idea what you are messing with here, your father barely knew when he tried. Please."

I retrieve my finger, looking back to dad's journal. I seize it, tucking it under my arm as I look back to my reflection.

"Candice! Don't you dare! I've already lost your father and I cannot lose you," she screams, sobs beginning as she tries to pick the lock.

"But you have mom!" I shout back, feeling my eyes brim with tears. "You lost me when you forgot that you were supposed to care for me."

Just as the doors fly open, I do what I once saw my father do: I step through.

Wind rushes around me, a feeling like I am being sucked into an endless pool of water, and a darkness comes closer, consuming me like I am miniscule to its size. As the endless abyss before me has engulfed me whole and I cannot even seen the tips of my fingers, I fall into the darkness, my eyes softly closing as I let out a final breath.

Chapter 3

Where the hell am I?

What happened?

Looking around, I don't know what to think as my eyes scan the room. It's like a marble building, one you would see in Greece belonging to the gods, one mainly isolated from the outside except for three archways. Where I lay is in the middle of the structure, a white stone bed under me, just a plain rectangle that causes my back to ache.

How the hell did I end up here? As I sit up, right before me on the marble wall is a mirror, one that has a golden frame around the long mirror. I came here through the mirror in my house. I came here. If I am here and alive...my dad must be here and alive.

I get to my feet, the glad to see myself still clothed and in the same pair of sweatpants and old t-shirt. Pushing my fingers through my own hair, a deep sigh leaves my mouth as I look around at the outside. My body is still stiff, my mind wondering off to the question of how long I was laying there, prone to any creature outside these walls.

A circle of trees surrounds me, thick evergreens causing me to wonder what is behind the trees. For sure I am somewhere. For sure some sort of civilization is clue. This whole thing makes me think of Minecraft, how a village will be my first place to go, to get food and a place to sleep. Walking over to one of the archways, I spot something that makes my stomach becomes tied up in knots. A storm is coming. Lightening can be seen. I either need to stay here or go and find some place to take shelter.

Right away I step out of the structure, looking in the opposite location of the storm as the wind picks up. This storm will not be one just to wait for it to pass, this one will be strong. I either head out into the unknown or wait it out. The first choice seems the best.

But who knows what creatures I could find here? What animals of predator and prey lurk around the next corner.

A loud crack of thunder and I'm walking away, straight for the tree line as my heart begins to pump faster. I just need to find somewhere safe tonight, and I hope I'm not placing my hopes too high.

The branches are low as they scrape my arms, the twigs pulling at my hair as my feet sink into the mud. This is not my ideal journey into the unknown. As for the temperature, every second it seems to be growing colder, the storm clouds nearing as I try and outrun it. Maybe I will be able to...but looking ahead, all I can see are trees.

For passing time, my whole concentration is upon dad's journal. I had tucked it under my arm before I am stepping through the mirror, but I awoke without it. Maybe it didn't make it, for that seems like the clear choice because I don't have it.

Another tall hill comes to view, one that I cannot see over. Sighing, I begin my ascend once more, thinking of my mother. As for what is up to, I have no definite idea, but I know she must be screaming over that mirror in agony. "Maybe she will look for me," I mumble, knowing that's a very clear answer. That's all she has done since dad left: look for him. Why only stop with dad? Why not look for your whole family as well? Pretty obvious to me.

"And just to think the next chapter of my life was about to start," I mutter to myself, thinking of college. I was going to go into interior design with a full ride scholarship to my dream school. I did do this to myself, stepping through that mirror because I could not take another second in the hollow walls of that house that has driven my mother to rely on an endless hope that my father will return.

A twig snaps.

My head twists around, the adrenaline kicking in as I can feel my heart beating fast. Maybe an animal? The snapping was loud, too loud to be an animal unless a bear.

"What are you?"

I turn around, giving the woman a raised eyebrow as she inspects me. What am I? I'm human just like her...right. Unless this is some sick and weird alien community out here in the middle of nowhere.

"Who are you?" I ask, looking her over.

She's different, that's a definite issue right there. With golden locks pulled back into a braid she looks normal, not to mention just paler skin, but her eyes.... her eyes are so weird. They're blue, but bright, electric almost, swirling around as if water. Her eye color moves in designs. What the hell is going on here?

"So, the animal speaks."

"Animal?" I hiss, hearing the thunder only become louder. "Listen lady, or whatever you are, where am I?"

The woman cocks her head to the side, a pair of pointed ears displayed. Elf? Not Hobbit for sure. Why am I automatically assuming that she's some creature? For all I know she could be some lost cosplayer (though highly unlikely).

"Iduna," she replies. Iduna? How do you even pronounce that without some strange accent? "You must know, you speak the language."

"Yes, I've been taught English since I was a child," I reply sarcastically, thinking this woman to be mocking me, perhaps just playing a game.

She looks clueless. She looks uncertain of what to do. "Anglishe?"

I roll my eyes. "This is not funny!"

"You're speaking pretty good Idunian right now, creature," she comments. Idunian? It sounds like either some weird ice cream flavor or a Pokémon. Maybe a tech company? "Whatever that Anglishe is that you're speaking, it's clear Idunian."

I shake my head, not understanding. She's telling me I'm speaking some other language right now. "You know what, never mind, I just want to take shelter before the storm," I point out, looking over my shoulder to see the clouds coming closer as lightning strikes. The woman nods, motioning for me to follow her down the hill. I watch her as we walk. She looks human except for the ears...and the strange leather material of her clothes. Burgundy leather pants, a black shirt that looks like armor, and boots that also add to the look, she could be a cosplayer right now. This could all be some weird dream for all I know.

As we pass a small cliff, I only allow my jaw to drop as a small village lays before me. The village is carved into the cliff, homes located in the rock as staircases lead to other levels. There's glass windows, meaning this is not too strange of a world that I've set foot in. There must be some connection between my world and this one...right? Villagers stand outside their gray doors, many of the women dressed just as this one who leads me in, the men wearing dark pants and robes with hoods that cover their shirts. To me this looks like some warrior tribe.

"God, where am I?" I mutter to myself, onto to gain a raised eyebrow my way.

"What race believes in one Devine creator?" She asks, her face puzzled as I shake my head.

"It's an expression," I reply, following the woman onto the main streets of gravel that the village has, some houses and shops built like cabins.

"What race would use their Devine creator's title in such a way that pays them no respect?" She's going to get me stressed out over a small saying soon enough.

The thunder booms, the ground shaking, and my eyes widening. "How bad will the storm be?" I ask as we pass by a small child and her father, the two both looking at me strangely. The children look normal to what a human would be, but their ears, their ears just give me the wrong impression. In books and movies many supernatural creatures appear human until they lash out, could this be the same case? The woman looks to a certain door up on the cliff. "Will it last long?"

"You must be from the more urban areas of the kingdom." What does she mean by that. "Out here the storms are presents from the gods that praise us for our hard work and devotion to them. We do indeed fear the storms, for the gods are to be feared, but they are hope for the land."

I look as a woman opens the door of her home, pulling out a bucket of what must be stone, engravings upon the item. "And many of us collect the water to enchant."

Enchant? Did I run into some cult here? "What for?" I ask, deciding to take this village as a new culture that I'm experiencing rather than something to be afraid of. Hell, I am scared. I'm scared that I don't know where I am or anybody here.

"You really don't know. Where were you raised? By the oceans?" I guess to be raised by the oceans is bad around here, seen as a negative comment to give someone. "We enchant it for the purposes of potions. You do know we sorceresses sell the potions at the end of every two months. We head up to the nearest urban city and sell them there."

My God. Magic. They do spells upon the water and sell them. Magic. They actually practice magic and not some sort of science that is kept hidden.

"I'm sorry, I forgot, I thought you were elves."

The woman stops dead in her tracks, her eyes becoming a darker blue as the thunder roars. Eyes fall upon me as I know I've done something bad. "Those evil creatures may have been part of our ancestry, but we despise that half of us, creature, we are not cold killers and deceivers as they are." Her tone informs me well to never compare her to an elf again. "The treason that they have committed, the betrayal, their suave personas as they believe themselves to be better, have you no knowledge to never compare anyone to an elf?"

So, elves are evil suddenly here. The only elves I can picture are the ones from fantasy books and movies, where elves are seen as porcelain and pristine dolls, how they are sophisticated, and the race known by their beautiful music score. "I'm sorry," I reply, feeling the wind shift as many decide to head indoors. "So, what is in the city? Markets?"

The woman cocks her head to the side. "You ask a lot of questions for someone your age."

I ignore her last comment and look around. All I can see are trees and trees, a small path heading through a patch of them. I'm guessing the nearest city is far away. "Unlike someone who lives by the ocean or those who live in town, we prefer a simpler life without the luxuries."

What does she mean by that? Do they have car? They have glass windows so that must mean something. Right?

"What luxuries?"

"We better head on in," she replies, not answering my question as the drizzle of rain begins.

Walking up a staircase, eyes are still focused upon me. The woman leads me into one of the houses, one that smells like herbs.

The first room is different than what I would expect. With stone walls and wooden flooring, that's not the part that makes me raise an eyebrow, but the plants hanging from the ceiling in bunches as they give off an herbal scent does. Jars lay on wooden tables, filled with different smelling spices or even liquid, little heads on string around the jars. All over are small artifacts that look like they belong in some fortune teller's home.

"Follow me."

And I do, passing under an arch and into a smaller room with a wooden table, candles lighting the room. "So, creature, what are you known as?" The woman grabs from the table an old book, the pages turning brown, and the leather worn.

What do I say? Human? "A werewolf who hasn't shifted?"

Werewolf? Since when did werewolves exist? Then again, if elves and all the things here exist, so can werewolves. I even just did portal travel into another realm, these things should not surprise me at all for I should expect them.

"Because if you are, I'm going to have to ask you to leave, we are not fans of your kind."

"I'm not a... werewolf," I state, the phrase feeling foreign. Never did I ever think I'd be saying something absurd like this. "I'm human."

The book drops, landing on the floor as the room grows painfully silent. She knows of humans.

"Have you met one of us before?" I ask. If she knows what a human is, maybe she's run into one before, maybe she met my father. The woman picks up her book from the floor, her eyes widening as I have no clue what she's going to say.

"I've heard of one, a male. I've also heard of the stories."

"The stories?" I ask, watching as she takes a step away from me. Is she afraid of humans? What's wrong with humans?

"Of the ancient humans, the ones that hunted the supernatural and believed we were demons." The woman sets the book back down on the table, grabbing from under the table something I cannot see. In seconds I'm thrown across the room, my back colliding with the wall as I'm held a foot from the floor by some force.

The woman approaches, holding out a dagger, holding it so that it points to my neck. "Why are you here? A hunter? Your kind is supposed to be world's away, separated by magic." Supposedly I'm the enemy. So, our world was cut off by magic. What is going on?

"What are you talking about?" I ask, my heart thumping in my chest as fear takes over. "I came here to find my father."

I'm released, my knees colliding with the stone floor as I take a gasp of air. She is strong with whatever power that is. "I came here to find my father who spent his life trying to come here. He came about eleven years ago."

The woman raises an eyebrow as she pulls out a chair, taking a seat as I stay on the floor. "How do I know you're not here with others of your kind, to kill."

Getting to my feet, I get the hint she wants a chat. The thunder roars outside, the downpour beginning as the room becomes darker. "Because I want my father back. I want to meet the man that raised me for so few years that I can barely remember."

"I cannot help you find him, no one in this village can. We hold no records nor get any news from the outside world. We like to be isolated from the rest."

The rest? What else is out here? Besides the wolves and whatever this race is, what other races are there to be seen? Should I fear them?

"The rest?"

She doesn't reply, simply getting up and moving to the next room. Following the woman, I'm surprised to see a bedroom, one with a simple oak bed stand, a handwoven blanket upon the matters, and a wooden wardrobe. "The only place you can get your information is the capitol, and you're lucky, tomorrow there is a group leaving. In four days you should arrive there, and I'll make sure that I get you into the archive of the palace."

"The archive?"

"There's a room holding all the events in the past years of strange things that have happened. A fellow villager now works there since marrying a wolf."

So, I'll have to get into the palace of some King and Queen. "Why are you helping me? I don't know if it's because you are just this n-

"I'm helping you because my kind sees humans as a curse. The longer you are here the longer you put yourself at risk of death." My heart literally stops. They could kill me here. "I do not want to watch a young girl like you die brutally, so I'm going to help rid you of our lands quickly. Once at the palace I will leave you with some money." So, she's going to help. "Tomorrow I'll get you dressed like a normal person here and we head out early. If anyone asks, you are a werewolf who has not yet shifted."

Just as another roar of thunder shakes the house and makes me jump, an image flies through my mind. An image of beautiful eyes that seem to hold the universe within them as they stare at me. Whoever owns those eyes, they must be one lucky person.

Just as the woman looks back to me, she holds out her hand.

I take it, not prepared for what happens next as I'm shocked, a wave running through my body as I once again fall into the darkness. But not before those eyes pass through my mind one last time.

Chapter 4

"You will need this," Soka explains as the last string is pulled tightly on the corset. Sucking in a deep breath as my ribs feel like they are about to break under pressure, Soka pulls out a slim and long dagger. Simple and sharp, I can see my reflection in the polished metal. "For protection. Many unholy things happen within the palace walls." I nod, taking in my appearance in the mirror before me. Another mirror to bring back the memories of my mistake. An intentional mistake as I know I must accept that.

I had no idea what I did would work, nor did I think I would step through.

So here I stand now, dressed in a corset that punctures my ribs as the thin fabric of a dress is slid over my head. Hunter green, the material a tad worn as I rub my fingers against it. Hitting the floor with a little room to show the brown boots, I actually don't mind the attire, except for the fact it is a little itchy. Soka pulls my hair back into a simple braid, explaining that women within the palace walls and conjoining city still dress formally like this. Explaining that the nobles and royals wear silks and bit more modern gowns, I will look like nothing less than a villager from the werewolf community off the coast of Iduna's second largest island.

"Thank you," I express, taking the dagger and sliding it into my boot as Soka informs it is to stay hidden. Along with that I'm told the rules of how to look, how my chin must be held, to never walk faster than those dressed in silks and jewels, to never let my dress go above my ankles, and to never ever dare put my hair down. Why not to put my hair down? Soka explains only the ladies of the night wear their hair down.

Informed that the ride will be long to the Capitol, my thoughts are placed upon my father. There is a chance I could find him out there. There's a chance I could see my father once more.

"So, does the King mind commoners in his library?" I ask, remembering I'll be in the palace and in a library to search for records.

Soka shakes her head. "He has a private library just as massive, the one you will be in is open to those who give reason to be in there. Luckily for you, for I do believe my gods have shown you mercy though your kind hunts their creations, I know the man who operates the flow of who comes and passes through that library."

"Does the King have a Queen and children?" I ask.

"The King is new, yet to choose a bride, though many think it will be another werewolf from one of the three islands located off the west shore. He is barely even twenty-two."

"Young for sure."

Soka nods. "He took the title only seven full moons ago, his father had passed eight years ago, and his mother ruled until sickness overtook her. Now his parents are with the gods and I pray they are still respected by their people who live on."

So, religion is one important of a thing here. The way Soka talks about her gods and everyone else's just likes me know I'd better not ever insult them.

As the pale morning sun rises over the trees, I take my spot on the wagon, seated next to a chest filled to the brim with magical potions and a small boy who plays with a horse made of field grass. Looking back upon the village, I'm left only to wonder when the next time I'll be back as it becomes only a smaller structure the more time passes bye. Maybe I will return one day. Maybe I will never see these homes again.

For another three hours I just stare upon the views of trees and mountains, missing the technology that would aid me in my boredom. For many minutes I just run the fabric of my dress between my fingers, thinking of my mother and friends who I have now left behind. I left behind a boyfriend as well, one of two years, one who I've grown to appreciate more and more every day we were together. And now, as I sit here, this is the first time I think of him, of Nicholas. I didn't even spare him a thought when I disappeared into the mirror. I was so consumed by the thoughts and memories that I tried to still hold of my father that I just let everything else go from my mind.

In another hour I'm closing my eyes, listening to the horses as their hooves dig into the trail. Soka talks for many minutes to multiple people as five wagons are ahead of the one I'm on. She talks of herbs and ways to make different potions. From what I've gathered she does medical potions for sleep, sickness, and many others that she prices highly. It's interesting to hear about as I imagine lying on my back in my bed, wanting to have the TV on as I know I'm about to leave for college.

But will I ever go home? If my father is here he must know a way to return. But then again, my father has not returned for years. Is there even a way back home? Knowing just the simple lays of portals or whatever you would call it, where there is an entrance, there is an exit. Think of it, in any story or game involving portals, how you can go back and forth between the worlds. The orange and blue portals, how one allows you to enter and the other to exit. For all I know I could be stuck in a pocket universe. Hell, I don't even know what to do if I find records of my father. Or even if I don't find records of a human. This was his life's work, meaning he had a purpose to do this trick with a mirror. But did he really think there was a world that he would be taken to?

For lunch we have a simple meal of some sort of bird I've never heard of as its paired with bread. Ale is passed around on some wagons as I'm left with a small bottle of wine and a pitcher of water to share with three others here. Including the small boy beside me, there's two others, both females, a tad younger than me.

Both bearing sleek and black hair that's pinned back, maroon dresses, and their eyes just like Soka's, they spare me glances every now and then. Sometimes whispering among themselves only to giggle, I know it's about me, how I'm referred to as the pitied wolf. I guess being werewolf and unable to shift is some curse.

"Excuse me, but have either of you been to the palace?" I ask, wanting to be friendly and strike up a small chat.

They ignore me and look away.

"Don't mind them," the small boy beside me comments. He speaks. I haven't heard him say a single word since we left and now he speaks. Shy perhaps. "My mother says they are just going through a phase where they disrespect those they should actually bow to."

They have a right to ignore me. The fact that my kind would hunt theirs according to Soka gives them every right. But what they don't know can't harm them. Right?

"Who should they bow to?" I ask, finding that this child will be my companion for the journey ahead.

"The one who wears the crown."

"Do they not bow to him?"

The boy offers me a small smile, shaking his head to signal that the girls do not. "My mother says they objectify them."

I almost choke on my own air as he says that sentence. Not only does his vocabulary surprise me for a child his age, but how he says objectify. It makes me think of how men objectify women as something to holler at and use for personal gain without realizing that these women have a mind and body of their own. The way he says that statement makes me imagine these two girls think of their King as just some piece of meat. I know it happens, but it's so weird to hear it.

"That's because he is a beautiful as the heavens," one of the girls state, paler than the other as she drops in on the conversation.

"And as deadly as hell itself," the other points out. "They say he holds a power only the gods could have."

How they describe this young King makes me wonder if I should be scared when I enter the palace. How they despise him in my mind makes me wonder just what he has done to be claimed as some vicious monster they both should fear and see as beautiful.

"His mother was so beautiful that countries fought over her."

Helen, that's who I think of. The woman and Queen who Paris stole and took back to Troy to become his wife, only for the great city to be burned to the ground from the inside.

"And now they say the gods plan to bless him with a wife and Queen more pure and beautiful than the Great Queen herself."

Now these two are just talking weird gossip that I would expect from A Midsummer's Night Dream or something else Shakespearian. The two girls return to their own conversation and I am once again left alone to wonder who this King is and what he has done to make him so appraised and feared. Did he kill? Did he cheat? Threaten? Demolish? Was he like Rome when they desolated Carthage? Was he like Caesar when he took over his own country by force? Was he like Alexander the Great when he conquered lands before he even reached the peak of his age?

The two girls state that the gods are to bless him with a wife like none other. Will she be like the wife of Hades, trapped in a dark abyss where her pure soul is constantly tempted by the wicked? Will she be beautiful as they say she is to be? Pure? Why do these people talk so strange when their world was once mine and still is in the same time continuum?

By nightfall we have set up tent, a small fire being lit as a stag is taken from the woods by hunters to be fed upon. As I sit on a log and stare into the fire, something seems to pull me in, to entice me as I create a certain tunnel vision, forgetting the world around me.

It's as if the flames create a dance, the individual flames of the hot fire dancing in a battle, only to conjoin as one. Once the row separate, they begin again, battling out another dance of the fates as the sparks fly high into the night. Looking up to the night sky, I see the familiar constellations. I see Ares, the Little Dipper, and so many others my mother had books upon. She believed my father was even researching the stars for the trick of his career. As I catch a glimpse of a shooting star, my mind seems to shut down as a certain image once again floods my mind.

Those eyes. The eyes that hold the entire universe within two orbs, all the colors and beauty held still as time ceases to exist. A true wonder of the world.

"Wolf."

I look back to the people around me as one of the men who hunted the stag hands me a wooden plate with a slice of meat and small scoop of rice. I somehow miss the cooking of my mother. Though her cooking was rare to experience a usually tasted as you would expect from a child's first-time cooking, I miss it.

As the night drags on my mind constantly shifts as I try and rein age those eyes that makes me wonder who owns them.

Once cocooned within a thick blanket, I shut my eyes for the night, focusing on the heartbeat within my chest as I wonder what my mother is up to. What my mother is feeling. I left my mother all alone with no one around. Sure, she's used to no family around her as she travels and even forgets she has a growing daughter at home, but she always knew she had someone to return home to. She always knew she had someone to make the house feel full. And now, she knows she has no one to return to. She knows the house is empty.

I feel the pull into the darkness, my mind drifts off into the night as I allow myself to fall asleep once more in a new world. A world I have yet to comprehend even a fraction of.

The rows of chairs are packed from front to the cheapest seats, people dressed in their finest jewels and brands as the music plays lightly in the background. I'm different than the rest, yes, dressed in a fancy gown that sweeps the floor and a pearl necklace, but I'm different. No one notices me, no one spares me a glance. No one sees me.

I move on my own, headed down one of the isles as the lights begin to dim. Paper can be heard as people from the press ready their pens and others turn on their massive cameras. As I take my seat next to an elderly couple, I look to the stage where the velvet curtains are shut, and chatter turns to whisper.

Silence as the lights go off. Not a single movement can be seen or heard as my eyes watch the curtains pull back to reveal a beautiful woman.

Her diamond necklace sparkles under the stage lights, a bright smile upon her face as she welcomes the crowd. Beginning with a small joke, the audience offers a joyful laughter that is followed by a tense atmosphere. Throwing her arm up, the first trick is revealed and suddenly, in a puff of silvery smoke, a man appears out of nowhere, a tuxedo tailored to his form and a bow tie fixed to perfection. Both people wear wedding rings, the man with a simple silver band and the woman with a silver band where a massive diamond sits upon it.

Trick after trick the audience claps, and the couple takes a bow, sometimes adding in jokes or even comments about their family. A small daughter. One sitting backstage as she awaits her daddy to tuck her into bed like every night.

I know this night. I've known what night this was since the moment I was in the room.

The final trick is brought out, the rectangular device covered by a silk fabric.

The man explains the piece, how it will be a gateway to a new era of magic tricks and ricks. He explains how this trick will define his career, if it was truly a success as many people claimed, or a doomed path as few predicted.

I remember this. I remember seeing my father disappear and never come back.

And I watch it again, as he disappears into the mirror and the room is silent.

My mother turns the mirror around in a complete circle, showing the slim mirror as the crowd is in awe.

But seconds turn into minutes and worry floods the auditorium.

Minutes turn into a lifetime as I watch the theater crumble before my very eyes and instead I look out upon a reflection of myself.

In a simple room with four white walls and one mirror before me, I look at my reflection, the scared girl before me as a tear slides down my face. I lost everything that night. I lost my father. I lost my mother. I lost my childhood with happy moments I will never get to explore.

Closing my eyes, I allow the dream to carry on, only wanting to wake up and see another sunrise. And maybe I will. Maybe I will see another sunrise, but not just one where I wake up a strange land, but one where I wake up in my bed and head downstairs to see both my parents enjoying a cup of coffee as they laugh and smile as they once did.

Maybe one day everything will be normal. Maybe one day I'll get my Christmas wish and birthday wish from over eleven years of the same wish and dream.

Allowing myself to live the dream a bit longer, I soon stir, knowing another day I a strange land is upon me. And yet, as scared as I should be, a certain feeling within my chest that makes it strain makes me excited for the day ahead.

Chapter 5

T he last and third day approaches as we spend the morning packing up camp. The weather last night was a storm, the winds blowing harshly as the rain hit the material of the tent like bullets. Soka said it was her gods, her gods telling her to get me out of her village's life, to leave her people alone.

As I throw the last sleeping pad made of feathers and a thin cotton sheet onto the wagon, the small boy who has become my friend tugs on my sleeve. "Alwin, what can I help you with?" I ask, sitting down on the wagon's edge as he follows.

"Udela says you are to be gone tomorrow night, to stay in the city."

Udela is his older sister, one of the two twins. She's the older of the two, Coventina being the younger of the two. I was told Coventina was named after their religion's goddess of the water, the one Soka says is warning her to get me out of here.

"I have to, I have to find someone," I explain, feeling his small hand take mine as everything else is loaded up. "But maybe we will see each other again?"

Alwin looks up to me with watery eyes, giving me a soft nod.

For seven hours we ride, the weather growing colder by the hour. Soon enough I'm being given a thick blanket to share, one that Alwin and I huddle under, my hands shaking. "Is the road to the Capitol usually this cold?" I ask Udela, watching as she puts on a fur coat.

"It is winter up in the Capitol, they are located higher above the sea, in four full moons it should begin to heat up," she explains, turning right back to her sister as I'm left to the company of a small boy once again.

Soon enough small villages once spotted every two hours ago become more consistent. Now, as we ride past, the villages grow in size and shorten in distance between each one. Eventually I'm spotting bigger houses, less farming, and even children running through the streets as they play. Nothing looks the same as back home, the once modern houses I was so familiar to seeing, now everything is made of white brick, shingles upon the roofs, and unique shapes making me only more interested in what the Capitol will appear to be.

I have many ideas. I can image tall walls just like the city of Troy, beautiful marble building like Athens, and upon a hill just like Sparta.

"Wolf, we are to be there before sunset, do you have everything you need?" Soka asks, walking over to the wagon as I remember myself who I am to be from here on out. To ever have hope of finding my father or going back home, I will have to take on this new identity. "Candice?"

"I have everything I need," I reply, watching as she nods and heads to another wagon, leaving me all alone in a strange world.

Before sunset I can already see the hill of the Capitol, the massive marble walls surrounding the city as a small town circles the gates.

Soka told me within the walls are the wealthy homes, those of mer-chants, Royals, military officials, and much more who can pay for the higher living conditions. The castle can be seen as well, overlooking the town's below as it stands high, tons of towards with different heights coming from the center as the windows are beautiful, the deign just breathtaking.

"History says that the elves of the Third Age built the castle for the rightful rulers," Alwin explains as the cold air nips at my skin once again. Looking at the castle more, I can see the snow upon the roof, covering even the walls with ice sickles hanging low. The fields around the walls are surrounded in a thin layer of snow. "Winter has just begun, meaning the fields are to be dead longer than a month."

I nod, looking upon the child. "What do they grow out here?"

"Some do food, others grow items like cotton and even silk."

"Silk?" I ask, looking upon the fields where simple yet beautiful houses are placed. Silkworms are how silk is made, yet here, silk is someone farmed.

"Candice!" Soka calls out, shaking her head in the distance. I guess that's a topic she doesn't want me expanding upon. Maybe because it's different here. No doubt it is since these people can use some freaky magic.

The closer we get to the gates the more my body begins to shake in nervousness. It has the gates of Troy, the marble buildings of Athens, and (from what I've heard from Soka) the army of Sparta.

As we pull before the massive set of marble double doors, guards come out to search us, their armor a shiny silver, maroon colors under as a flag they also carry is a dark maroon with a silver wolf.

"When we stop I'll walk you to the royal library," Soka explains as the carts start up again, taking a seat beside me as my mother flashes through my mind. I wonder how she's doing, what she's up to, what she's doing to get me back. Yes, I'd like to go back, to head off to college and make memories, but I made my decision, and it has its consequences. Who knows if I'll ever be able to go home.

That's why I want to find my father, to see him once more as we search for an escape.

As we pass through the gates, I'm caught in amazement as I take in the buildings around me, white stone appearing like stone covering the ground as fresh green grass plays in certain locations where beautiful and massive trees with silver leaves are, the buildings made of white marble, the houses looking like the type a design would make in Greece for some billionaire's weekend escape. But what catches me off guard is the castle, the massive building that causes a gasp to leave my mouth. Tons of towers span towards the sky, glass windows tall and thin, letting in plenty of natural light. The doors to the palace are up a set of marble steps upon a hill, the castle about half a mile away, truly beautiful with perfection. I can what Alwin meant by the elves crafting the castle.

"Candice, come with me," Soka informs as we come to a small intersection where other carts also heading towards a market intersect us.

Jumping from the cart, I look to Alwin, offering him a simple goodbye. He waves bye, hoping me luck and my gods be with me. "Follow me."

And I do, weaving into small alleyway after small alleyway, the cold making me have flashbacks to last winter, how I shoveled the driveway while my mother was off in India, looking at different shrines for clues as to my father's mirror. "Where is the library?" I ask, the light later of snow barely crunching beneath my feet.

"See the massive building to the left of the castle, the ceiling made of glass?" I do. The roof is a massive window, angled, looking right up at the stars. "It's used for astronomy as well, many scribes using the library to write through the night. My people say the stars shine so bright at night in that room that the spirits of the gods flood the room."

"That's where I'll go?" I ask. "Where will I sleep? What will I eat?"

"I promised you a small amount of help. The man who works there now will take care of you. He owes me a favor."

"For what?" I ask, approaching the massive doors of the library. A thin bridge on the second floor connects the library to the palace, an arch under as people walk bye.

"I healed his daughter five weeks ago of an illness."

I nod, watching as the doors open for us and the scents of herbs meet my nostrils. Chandeliers hang from the ceiling that's not made of glass, a small room where the entrance is, the walls painted with a light blue tint as marble pillars spread across the area. A huge opening leads us into the library, rows after rows of books on white shelves spanning to the top of the floor's ceiling.

"Four stories filled with books. The fifth is where the ceiling is," Soka explains as a small opening on the first floor lets me see an area where all the stories open up, allowing me a view of the gray yet bright sky. "The man I am speaking of will offer you both a place to stay and food. I trust him. He is a good man, one dedicated to his Moon Goddess."

What I recall is the Moon Goddess is the werewolf deity.

"Follow me."

I do, coming to a staircase as we climb the first four stories. "Where will we find him?" I ask.

Soka leads me to the top floor, the floor covered in desks with simple chairs, the walls covered with books. "He is an astronomer, reading the stars for the Moon Goddess' plan. Also, a royal consultant for the King."

Two men are on the floor, one with longer gray hair, his blue eyes still bright, and a beard spanning to his mid-torso. The other is dressed in what would be a simple toga, his white hair trimmed short, no beard, and dark brown eyes that seem to convey a mysterious feel.

"Travon!" Soka calls out to the latter, the man in the toga turning around with a massive book in his hand.

"Merchant Soka, many greetings from the gods," Travon greets, a smile crossing his aging face as his eyes meet mine. "A friend?"

"One in need to help," Soka informs, Travon walking up to us as his shadow stands over me. He's tall for sure. "May we speak privately?"

He nods, Soka turning from me as they walk off towards a distant corner. No doubt she's explains to him either my situation or that she wants me dead before the morning sun.

I'm left to my thoughts as they reach the shadows of a corner, whispering among the other as I place my hands behind my back. Taking the time given, I head for the bookshelves, surprised to see everything in English. Weird. Though thinking back upon it, Soka said I spoke her language perfectly and I had no idea I was not speaking English.

The Age of the Darkest Blood

Sounds like one hell of either a boring or exciting book. No doubt history though, something that causes me to shake my head. Probably something to deal with elves or something.

"Most women wouldn't dream of picking that book up."

I look over my shoulder, surprised to spot Travon there with Soka beside him.

"Merchant Soka has expressed your situation and the name you are searching for. I am happy to provide you with a home, but the records you will not find here."

"Where can I find them?" I ask, feeling my body heat up in stress.

"In the castle. I can get into the records room tomorrow before the King orders the doors sealed. Do not fret."

Within another ten minutes I find myself in the company of a stranger, someone barely a friend told me to trust. He explains to me we are to head to his place soon, a simple house about a five-minute walk away, the second story of a building where his mate keeps it filled with plants. I remember Soka explaining on the way to the Capitol that a mate is the soul mate, a term I still believe is a silly idea. No two people are perfect together.

Yes, my parents were happy together, but they were not perfect. No one is perfect of each other. Not to mention the idea of far picking out who you are to be with for the rest of your life is just too childish to truly believe. Much less even think of.

We head out once more, leaving the library as Travon explains to me I am to follow him tomorrow into the room of records, to aid him as we look for my father's name or even recognition of a human out of place here. I'm also told the story of me being a wolf not yet shifted is perfect, how no one could ever tell unless my blood was to be smelled if I was bleeding.

Yet that frightens me. What would happen if someone found out I was not of this world, but the one where their predators still lived on? Would I become the prey, hunted down for game? Would I become what these people once were to centuries before my life? I don't even know how much time passes here as it does back home. What if I get back home to discover I've been gone for forty years and my mother is on her death bed or already gone? How many years has my father been gone for here?

As I look over my shoulder once again, I spit the castle, a place that just reels me in. Something about it has a pull upon me, my heart thumping in my chest the longer I look upon it. Whatever it holds, I know there is something drawing me to it. There must be something that causes my nerves pick up and my heart pound as my fingers become tingly.

"Candice?" Travon asks, pulling me back to reality.

"Yes?" I reply, looking back from the palace as he gets the hint something is going on.

"One thing you must promise me tomorrow is very important."

"What it is?" I welcome, understanding completely as I know the risks at state. Of me being found out to be a human in a world filled with myths.

"You must not make eye contact nor speak with anyone...if you do, I am afraid I cannot protect you from whatever happens."

"Why?" I ask, taking one last glance at the castle.

"Because I feel as if the Moon Goddess is warning me of something. Something that deals with you and that castle."

"What do you mean?" I ask, raising an eyebrow as my heart falls to my stomach.

"I mean that something is bound to happen tomorrow. Something fate has set in place."

Chapter 6

S tunning.

Magnificent.

Halls with ceilings that seem to grasp the sky, marble pillars going just as high with intricate carvings, and windows that seem to be endless as my footsteps echo across the marble halls.

Every turn causes another small gasp to escape my mouth, how each room has its own unique spin upon the ostentatious design of the palace. "Are there not too many palaces where you come from?" Travon asks, his voice low as a maid passes bye, avoiding eye contract as Travon said to do.

"Not particularly. There are quite a few famous ones, but I've never been to one this immense and captivating," I explain, looking to the ceiling as paintings of different shapes of the moon, stars, and what I assume much be these people's deities. "None this breathtaking."

Travon nods, leading me to a more secluded staircase, spiraling up in a tower. "It's four stories up, the records room is one that will also astonish you." Nodding, I follow Travon, my feet hitting the hunter green dress that I wear as I remember what Travon taught me: shoulders squared, head tilted high, and make no eye contact whatsoever. I need to play the part of someone with good motives to be here but draw no attention to myself.

My mother had a way about drawing in attention. She practiced how she would walk, the particular placement of her feet when they met the floor, how her arms would move, how she would smile. That was a talent of her's: to draw attention whenever she wanted. She was able to reel my father in that way, fascinating him from the moment he spotted her. She led him on just for fun until she realized her true feeling for him. The media claimed they were a match made in heaven. The media said nothing could go wrong. The media sold a lie to the public, but of course they knew nothing of what could transpire.

"When we enter the records room, I do not know how many people will be there already but stay close by me and we shall find the name of your father."

"Do you think he will be in the records? Hell, I don't even know how long my father has been here for."

Travon shrugs his shoulders. "I've never heard of dimension traveling, my dear, but if your father did anything, it would be in here."

As we finished climbing the stairs, another hall lies before us, twists and turns taking us every way as I find myself looking outside upon a garden. I thought I'd seen some of the world's biggest gardens, but nothing could ever compare to this one. It's long and wide, bushes marking paths as flowers and authentic trees and planted along, fountains and ponds running everywhere. There are some women out, dressed in flowing pastel purple dresses as they take care of the plants.

"Those are nymphs, they take care of the castle grounds," Travon explains, expanding my horizon on just how many creatures of myth live here.

"What of vampires?"

Travon raises an eyebrow.

"Most reside within the human world..." He pauses. "We get along with them, but the elves do not wish to associate themselves with the vampires. The elves find them to be uncivil and always looking for trouble."

"And do you have dragons?" I ask, clasping my hands behind my back as a massive oak door is not too far away.

"They reside within the mountains about a week's journey from here. Dragons are tricky creatures. Either they destroy or keep to themselves."

I think of the Hobbit, how Smaug was one who destroyed and set a president for most of people's interpretations upon dragons. In Beowulf the dragon was greedy as well, ending Beowulf's journey. The books depict dragons as evil, ancient drawing with dragons burning down castle or taking a princess for the prince to soon rescue.

"Keep silent in here, I will nod when you are to speak," Travon orders, looking back to the door as he waves his hand.

The doors open, revealing a room that causes me to think of the Tardis. Small on the outside and big on the inside. It's as if this massive castle on gets bigger as you set foot inside.

I follow Travon, the sunlight streaming in as I'm amazed. Book shelves line the walls, sliding ladders everywhere, stairs to a second and even third story as only more folders and books lie before us. The smell of old books causes my heart to warm. The floor is polished to perfection, a crest of the Iduna Kingdom in the center of the floor as guards are on each side of the door.

Few people are here, most dressed in fancier attire as they skim the shelves for certain records.

"There are three record libraries in the palace. This one is for primarily historical records that even date back to when Selene created the werewolf race. But also, in this library is a small list of unusual people that have crossed this land, the kingdom keeping a knee eye upon them."

So, he thinks this is where we shall find the news of my father.

Travon leads me up the stairs, to the second floor as we pass by book shelf after book shelf. Soon, we are hidden from the public eye, Travon skimming every shelf for whatever we are exactly looking for.

He pulls out one of the books, a silver ribbon tied around to keep the contents in. Untying the ribbon, he opens the book, golden dust escaping as he flips through the pages.

"How long ago did your father vanish?"

"Eleven years in my world," I remind him, crossing my arms as I look around for anyone close bye. "His name was William."

Travon skims the book, heading back further as his fingers trace the countless pages.

William was his true name, but he adapted a new one when he took the stage and the cameras were all on him. He loved magic, he did not believe it was just science that the world had not discovered yet. My father believed magic was of its own essence.

"What would he have done here?"

I barely even knew my father. How could I guess what he would do here? But he loved magic, and if this was his final trick, the only explanation would be to explore.

"Travel the land. If anything, he would have come here as well."

Why wouldn't he come here? The Capitol of the world he had searched for countless years.

"Peculiar travels are not common, but I can try and find him."

Hours later and countless books as well, I sit against a bookshelf, my eyes barely peeled open as Travon is one row down, still searching for the name of my father to appear.

Would William even be used? Sure, it was his true name, but would he have used his true name in a magical world. Would he of rather used his magician name in this magical world?

"Can I offer you another name?" I ask, Travon looking over his shoulder to me. He nods. "Heka."

"What is that name?" Travon asks, a tone in his voice that makes me wonder what is wrong with the name.

"A country in my world called Egypt, it's the world for the personification of magic, like the ancient practice of it."

Travon shuts the book, quickly putting it away as he rushes to me. Grabbing my arm, he pulls me with him, up another flight of stairs as my heartbeat quickens.

"Have you heard the name?"

Travon nods. "One of a kind."

I raise an eyebrow as Travon's hands begin to shake, letting go of me as he skims the rows of records.

Just as he placed his finger upon one, the atmosphere of the room begins to tense, a tunnel-like vision occurring as my brain becomes light headed.

Travon lands his finger upon a sentence, skimming over and over it again as I take in deep breaths.

"Heka....the slayer of royal blood."

"What?!" I hiss, quickly pacing myself to where Travon stands.

He hands me the book, the heaviness surprising me as Travon points to the paragraph.

There's an illustration, one of a man portrayed with pale skin and poor clothes, pulling back upon an arrow in a black bow as one man sits upon a throne.

My father killed the man who wears a crown.

My father killed the King.

Looking up to Travon, I see fear in his eyes. I read the paragraph repeatedly, my palms becoming sweaty as I wonder what will happen next. My father shot and killed the past King right before the Prince's eyes. My father vanished into thin air before anyone could bring him to justice and has not been heard of for eight years. The son of the King swore to find my father and bring him to death along with all who reside with him.

Looking up to Travon, I see worry within his eyes. "I cannot let you stay within the palace walls any longer," he explains. "If they find out what you are, you will be beheaded as a warning to all."

"Who? Who would do so?" I ask.

"The King, the son of the King your father murdered."

He's right, I need to leave and leave fast.

Grabbing the book, Travon puts it away fast, motioning for me to begin walking back down the stairs as all I can concentrate on in my father. Why would he kill a man, a King? What made him murder a ruler? But even more important: where is he now?

Just as we reach the first floor, the doors shoot open, everyone within the room dropping to the floor and bowing. Travon grabs me, placing me beside him and taking me to the ground with him. We take the pose of everyone else within the records room, my heart skipping a beat as I can see shoes and a long robe trailing behind the individual. The robes are beautiful, white fur around a thick and silky maroon fabric. This man is royalty. But who?

He walks around the room, circling it as he passes bye every individual, getting closer to where I bow. If he does not linger too long, I shall be fine.

"Who has spoken the name?" What name? How would they even know what name was spoken? Were they just passing by or what?

He stops right before Travon.

"The name of a savage."

The voice. The voice of the man is what draws me in the most. The rich sound, baritone, beautiful to listen to. Yet it's a voice I would image not an angel to have, but a character such as Hades, one who is deceiving and dark. But a voice like that, one that holds so much authority and power, that I could get used to. Travon. I can sense it now. Travon is shaking. He is scared.

"The name of a murderer."

Heka.

My father's stage name. This man is describing my father. Is my father's stage name cursed now or something? Guards move forward as my arms begin to shake. They rip Travon from the floor and onto his feet, the individual taking a step back.

"Was it you?" He's talking to Travon. What will he do to him? Harm him? I am the one who got Travon into this mess. I am the one who is responsible for any wrongs to Travon or even Soka's kin for that matter. The individual steps away from Travon, the guards releasing him as he drops to the floor and back to kneeling.

Just as I think he's gone, I let out a sharp scream of surprise, my eyes wide as pain shoots through my arms.

Those eyes. The eyes that seem to hold the galaxy within them. Every constellation, planet, nebula, every aspect of the stunning universe held within those eyes as I could get lost in them for centuries. These are the eyes that have flooded my dreams.

The room falls still as no words are spoken, the only aspect that reminds me I am not dreaming is the pain of the guards holding me up.

"Or was it the small female..." The man states, his voice almost a whisper as he sounds as if it is hard to speak. "The one who no one would expect."

He takes a step forward, his hand reaching up, fingers softly brushing my cheek as my eyes expand. Shocks spread across every inch of skin he traces, my heart beating faster than a hummingbird's wings as I become speechless. He's inches from me, his guards no longer holding me as I stay up on my own. The way he looks at me, positions himself before me, how he barely even touches me, it all makes me wonder what is truly happening.

"Why would such an innocent creature speak such a discourteous name," he whispers, as if to himself as he comes closer. And I stay still, a soft breath escapes my lips as his tilts his head to the side.

And that's when I see it, the crown, the massive golden crown holing so much design and jewels that causes me to feel fear. This is the man that wants my father dead. This is the very man that would see me beheaded as a warning. This is the man Travon feared me ever running into.

This is the King, and I'm now in his domain.

He pulls back, walking around me as he scans me from top to bottom as his fingers dance across my shoulders for a second. It's as if he has a limitless longing to just be next to me, embrace me, see me, make sure I am not just a fixture of his imagination.

"Why would you say such a cursed name? Treacherous names should never leave those lips of yours."

He motions for his guards, the man laying a hand each upon my shoulder as I know trouble awaits me.

"It's as if you need to be taught a lesson."

My eyes widen, watching as a hint of mischief fills those eyes and I'm scared for my life.

"Do not fret, Astronomer Travon, she is in respectable hands now."

Respectable hands now?

It kicks in as he King turns his back to me, his guards ushering me out as this all feels like I have no control anymore. It kicks in that I am no longer in the hands of someone I trust to get me out of here, but in the hands of a man who will never let me leave.

And it's just a matter of time until he uncovers what I am.

Chapter 7

I follow the male, his robes trailing behind him as any movie would display a powerful king.

He looks like the perfect predator, how he walks, his chin held high, hands by his side, strides long, and never looking back at me. The crown upon his head only causes more fear to reside within my body. The fear of him uncovering not only who I am, but what I am. One small slip and I'm doomed, receiving the death to those he would have. After all, my father killed his father.

Why?

I have no clue.

The guards beside me don't add to my comfort as I'm forced to keep up with the male, pacing myself faster than usual as countless halls pass bye. How massive can this palace possibly get? It's truly a bigger on the inside, endless on in the inside as I'm overwhelmed by its beauty.

For now, I just walk behind the King, making sure to not draw any more attention to myself than I already have. After all, what more attention can I grab than the King's. After another five minutes of all I can hear is the sound of my feet across the marble floor, the King comes to a door, barely even sparing me a glance as one of the guards opens it up. Right away I wonder where I am now...if this is my end even.

"Are you coming, traveler?" The King asks, his voice enveloping me in some sort of spell.

I follow the King, deciding to keep my mouth shut as the guards stay behind, not bothering to follow as my skin pales.

This is not a room.

It's a balcony one the size of perhaps my whole childhood house's second floor. The marble floor stretches far and wide, a semi-circle as the railing is detailed with every curve. Furniture is out here, a ceiling over the balcony as a fire pit stands next to a couple of what I would call couches. But the view, the view is the most striking. It's one of the city beyond the palace, the white marble reflecting the beautiful pink and orange hues of the sunset as mountains lay in the background.

The sound of the doors shutting take me from my state of awe and throw me back into reality. Reality? Can this even be considered reality?

"Take a seat," the King motions, showing me a beautiful and comfy chair, just beside the railing, pushed up against it as if on purpose. The chair is high enough, that one simple push, and I'll be thrown over the railing and plummet to my death stories below.

I follow his words, taking a seat in the chair right against the railing. He moved the chair out here for a purpose, as seeing the group it was taken from is quite a way away from the railing.

The second I take a seat, I meet those eyes.

The eyes that hold the galaxies within them and make me in awe of space. It's as if every beautiful part of the universe has been thrown into his very eyes. How they change color amazes me, always holding a tint of purple, yet the endless specs of gold, vibrant green and blues, and even hints of gray only make me more amazed.

"So, what is the name of the woman who spoke that deadly name?"

I do not want to anger the King. I do not want to be thrown off the balcony and never make it home. Home, such a faraway term.

"Candice," I whisper, still afraid of this male as he seems hardly any older than me, yet the way he holds himself makes him appear only more mature and deadly. He's trouble. Yet that never stopped me before. Growing up I liked the thrill of doing something danger-ous or something my mother was against. Through middle school I did many things to try and draw my mother's attention and concern towards me, but rarely did that ever work.

"Candice..."

He is hinting at something, trying to get me to say another word or name. Do I give a last name? Do they have those here? Or does he want me to say another word...

"Candice, your Majesty," I respond, my voice soft as I decide to avoid eye contact, staring off to the side of the balcony, the drop off so close to me as the King leans forward.

Placing his hands on either side of the chair, he gets closer, his face inches away from my own as my body heats up. "Why are you so far from home, Candice?" He asks, his voice a mere whisper as shivers run down my spine as he says my name. "So far from the islands. From your kin."

"I-I'm going on an adventure."

That's the best I can do, quoting a movie as I cannot think of anything else to say.

"An adventure. Can you shift yet, Candice?"

Shift? I almost forgot I'm dealing with a world of the supernatural here.

"Not yet, your Majesty."

"You mean to tell me, that you, Candice, are a wolf less female going on an adventure? You have no form of protection," he explains, and there's a tone in his voice that threatens me. He is onto me. "Tell me, what will you do if a group of savage men try to violate you?"

My skin grows pale.

"I will fight."

"How? With no wolf you are useless," the King informs, getting even closer to me as my heart skips a beat. "How will you to text yourself."

I scream.

He's shoved the chair back, leaning back against the railing as one more inch and I will plummet to my death below. The small streets below, the people moving by as they pay no attention to the girl just dangling over that could possibly plummet to the ground below. I hold onto the sides of the chair, my knuckles turning white as I can feel gravity pulling upon me, wanting me to drop.

"Tell me, Candice, how will you protect yourself," he demands, his voice a growl as I meet his black eyes.

"With...with a sword," I say too fast to even acknowledge as my answer.

"A sword? A little thing like you fights with a sword?"

He wants answers, still holding me over the edge of the palace as I'm afraid for my very life.

He tilts the chair more, causing me to scream as I release my hands from the chair, making a bold move to grab onto the King's arms, the silk material giving me the information that the King is well built as I hold onto him for dear life.

"Please," I cry, not wanting to be dropped. "I can fight with a sword."

It's almost a truth. I did fencing as a child to teenager, quitting two years ago as I finally grew tired of it. My father fenced much in his youth, teaching my mother who got me started in the sport.

The King looks to where my hands are upon his arms, and I do not know whether to be scared or thankful that he has not flung me off him yet.

"I'm just traveling for fun, that is my adventure."

The King decides to grab me, wrapping his arms around my torso as the chair falls to the earth, probably breaking into millions of little pieces as the King sets me down upon the ground.

But as he removes himself from me, I almost hesitate to let go of him, wanting to be back and close to him. What has gotten into me? This man almost threw me off a balcony just to get simple answers from me. He's deranged. He's wacko, out of his mind and all that nonsense. Yet I still want to be close to him? How crazy am I becoming?

"Why did you say the name? That horrid name?" He asks me, cocking his head to the side as everything he does just seems to reel me in even more. "Every soul in this world know of that cursed name...if whispered within the palace walls, I will always hear it."

"Is...is it under a spell?" I ask, my voice soft as the King looks to me.

"Did you not learn that years age when I ordered the spell?"

"I... I forgot at the time..." I reply, hoping he will believe me as he decides to walk in a circle around me. He's interested in me. But why? What can I do to save myself though? What can I do to make him let me go and forget I even exist?

"Why did you need to look him up in the records?"

What do I say? That he is my father? That would be outright stupid.

That I was just going bye and wanted to know an oddly specific name? Too suspicious there. I must lie. I have to make up a story in my brain and spill it, hoping he will believe it.

"I..." I pause, watching as he stops walking and sits down, motioning for me to follow. Follow I do, standing before him with a story in mind. "That man killed my mother. I am on my adventure not for the sake of it, but because I want to find this man and bring him justice."

He raises an eyebrow.

"You are trying to find a man that has faded away from the face of the world?" the King asks, crossing his arms as I nod. "My men, my best men, have been trying to track him for years."

We both want to find him. We both want to find my father.

"I know things your men may not."

The King gets to his feet, grabbing my arm as he jolts me forward, looking down and into my eyes as my skin pales. "And what is that, little one?"

I have to sound confident.

"Add me to the race to find this man and you will find out".

Chapter 8

"Add you to the race?" He asks, raising an eyebrow as he approaches me. Yet I stand firm and in place, raising my chin in the process. "A female in a group of men as they search the realm?"

"Why not?" I ask.

"Who said I would add you to the race anyway?" The King questions, stepping a mere inch from me. His scent envelops me as my heart beats violently within my chest. How can he get me to feel this way after he almost let me fall off a balcony? "I have promised nothing to you yet."

"Then I no longer am needed here," I remark, looking over his shoulder and to the doors of the balcony. "Now, you should let me leave."

"Do you talk to your Ruler this way? Your Elders? I would be shocked if no one has threatened to banish you by now."

I stay silent. Not because he has truly won the argument, but because I believe one wrong slip up will make the King question of

I even have an idea what he is referring to. One slip up and he will think something is off with me even more than right now.

"That smart mouth of yours may get you in trouble one day."

I frown.

"Why should I add you? You could just tell me what to look for and be on your way back home."

He wants me here. I do not know why, but I know this man is not wanting me to leave anytime soon. Why? An odd feeling in my gut. That is all I know: an odd feeling in my gut that causes me to believe this man will not let me leave anytime soon. I have to get out of here. Soon he will begin to question me even more.

"Believe me, your men will have no idea what I am looking for."

Is it a lie? A lie to maybe find my father?

Maybe so. Maybe not. I know my father was a very smart man, one of believed in a signature mark. Every show he went to, mother told me he would carve a small marking into the doors of the changing rooms. Why? Mother always said he wanted to leave a mark for those who would one day replace him. No one has ever replaced my father. Still claimed the best magician of all history, year after year people still try and beat him, yet no one does.

"Believe me, you will need my help."

My help. My plan that I just developed minutes ago was to help these men find my father for me to find him as well. However, there will be a catch. Right as we are about to find my father, I will lead them astray after I gain their trust. Have them help me find my father. To find the man who I never got to live with as I grew up. The man who barely raised me. The man who knows how to get out of here.

Or at least I hope.

But he never came home.

Is there even a way home? Maybe my father is working on a way to go home? He has to be! He would have come home by now if he had a way!

"You are not the average woman, Candice," he states, his voice a soft whisper as he looks deep within my eyes. He's caught me in a trance once more. He's made me become lost in those eyes. "You talk to your King as if you are equal to me."

I should know better.

"I think you are a business partner. We are simply having a simple business deal. No one is a level higher during a deal for business."

The King scoffs, stepping a tad bit further as my skin pales. He's flush against me now, my heart beating faster than ever within my chest. "Impressive. That way of thinking for a woman."

I want to snap back at him. Yet these people are still living in a different time. Men and women are not equal. Sexism is everywhere here. Yet it seems as if he doesn't mind it, as if it's entertaining, as if, as he said, he is impressed. That's a good sign.

"Either I join the race to find this man or I leave."

A smirk crosses his face. What did I say? What caused him to appear smug, suspicious?

"Leave? You leave when I think it wise."

"Think it wise?" I ask, taking a step back, only for the King to grab my arm, pulling me back towards him as sparks fly though my arm.

"After all, you are in my domain."

My skin pales. He's not going to let me leave. But why?

What could make him want to keep me here? Consumed within my thoughts, by the time he has me right where he wants me, I'm stuck. Stuck within his grasp, I'm held against him, my back against his front as my heart skips a beat. His lips brush my ear as goosebumps form across my skin.

"Believe me, sweet Candice, my domain is tricky to leave." I swallow the lump in my throat.

"Am I added to the race to find him?" I ask, my voice stern as I am afraid it will crack.

"I have no reason to trust you."

I scoff.

"You are asking me to add a woman to the group who states she can aid me in finding a murderer." He lowers his head, his lips brushing my neck. "I have no reason to believe you could help me."

I'm afraid. Afraid to speak. Afraid of what he means. Afraid of why he will not let me leave.

"Trust me."

He pulls away, his body gone as I let out a silent breath. "Trust you?" He questions, walking in a circle around me as my fingers begin to shake. "The King trust a commoner?"

"Trust me."

He chuckles. "Trust me or I leave, and you will never have to see me again."

The King pulls away, staring down upon my figure as I find my hands begin to shake. As his eyes scan over my body, my body reacting right away as I feel my body temperature increase. His hands slide into his pockets, his crown catching the light of the sun as a knock occurs on the balcony doors.

"Your Majesty-

"Do you have a good reason to interrupt me?" The King snaps, facing the door as the guard is pale with fear.

"Your Majesty, word has reached the palace of an odd sighting, one in the rural lands, near the marble hall. Word has it of a magical spell."

My heart skips a beat.

Although I do not know anything about this realm, I know one thing for sure: the place the guard is describing...it's where I woke up.

Chapter 9

<hr>

"A magical spell?" The king asks, simply placing me by his side as the guard stands frail at the door, sensing that his King has become tense. "Those mountains are covered in creatures that cast spells, what makes you think it is of greater power?" He is annoyed that the guard has interrupted the quality conversation we were just having, but I fear that the King knows more about this marble hall than I would like. I came through that marble hall, through that mirror, and I have no doubt that that mirror is how my father also entered this realm. I fear that the King knows more than I would like, aware that this place is how my father entered the realm whose King he would slay.

His eyes meet mine, the universe reflected within darkening, as if some storm, a storm of darkness and destruction coming for the frail worlds is will crush with its power. "My King, the reports claim of some black lightening, striking the marble hall."

The King lets me go, something I had no idea he was capable of from the second he took me. Looking to the guard that shakes in his boots, the King cocks his head to the side, a smug smile pulling at the corner of his lips, fear sinking within my heart. "That is not just some marble hall," he begins, looking back to me as vibrant colors of orange and blue swirl around in his orbs. "It is a temple, one abandoned centuries ago, as well as the one that the cursed bastard came from." The King dismisses his guard, telling him to ready him a group of fifty men on horses, weapons, potions, and a thirst for blood ready in their souls as they will ride out at the end of the day. "Do not fret, Candice, I shall not need your assistance to find this murderer."

He thinks he has found my father, that this sudden activity is due to my father, but I know one thing for sure. I know that this lightening and the magical spells are all due to me. Why? How could I be certain if I have no true understanding on how this world works or what my father is up to? Because I know my father is a smart man, one that would not go back to that temple again...because if he had returned to that temple, he would have come home long ago. And now, with the King whose name I still have no idea of, he thinks he has found my father and that this temple holds the clues. I cannot let him go there without me, not because I plan to escape for that would be stupid to escape into the mirror while surrounded by these warriors the King has just ordered to get ready, but because I could get clues. I could see if that temple holds more than I would think, perhaps clues as to what my father was trying to do here, to study, to explore, and perhaps where he might be, or at least the path he has been traveling.

"That is where you are wrong," I state, standing up before the King as I know that I need to go to the temple. I need my answers and perhaps even an escape from this man's domain. "You need me, your majesty, because I am one of the few who can understand this horrid man's language."

What do I mean by this? I left my father's journal there, I had completely forgotten it in the temple when I had woken up. I was not holding it when I woke up there on that marble slab, but I know it must be there because I woke up with my clothes, my shoes, everything I had on me, meaning that the journal my father worked so hard on must be there too. I can read Idunian, Soka pointed that out, but I doubt these people will be able to understand English or even the hints of Arabic my father wrote in that journal. My father spending much of his time in the Middle East and out of that, a passion for the language of Arabic, even teaching me the language at a young age. The King and his men will have no clue how to read it, and while I may not tell them exactly what it says, it gives me the upper hand at finding my father, I can use it to my advantage and lead these men away from my father's trace while I can find him quicker.

"The language? So, you have come across this man's transcripts before?" the King asks, crossing his arms as he stands tall before me, his shadow falling over me as I know I have to think fast here. As a child I was a great liar, always able to get away with things. I got that skill from my mother.

I nod, taking a step back from the intimidating King, taking a seat once more upon one of the outdoor chairs, making sure this one is not too close to the edge. "When he came to my pack, he told our pack that he was to help us, a messenger from some sorceress," I lie, reminding myself that I am a werewolf, one that has not yet shifted. "I was a child then, one of the five he told he wanted to teach his language to." I am digging my grave here, more and more every word

I speak. "I learned his language very fast, my mother used to say I have a gift for languages, to be able to pick them up fast."

"Then he slaughtered the world you loved," the King pieces together, helping me remember the story of tragedy I made up to make us have some similar hate for the man that once tucked me into bed as a child. "So, you wish to be a translator?" I nod, telling myself to remain calm as my palms become sweaty and I look past the King's figure to see another figure in the doorway, this time a woman, one of ageless beauty. Her skin fair and not a blemish to be seen, steel blue hair pinned back in braids, bright golden eyes, and a figure of poise and strength, she looks to me, taking in my appearance as I remember Soka told me that only prostitutes have their hair down. I look like a prostitute to this woman, my hair framing my face due to the incident of being held over a multiple-story fall caused it to release.

The King notices where my eyes have gravitated towards, following their path as he turns his head to see the woman standing there. "Do you think she is a good choice for a translator, Lady Ebony?" He asks the woman who enters the room, the door shutting behind her has her dark blue dress sweeps the marble floor.

Lady Ebony looks to me once more, taking me in once again as her eyes scan over every feature of my body and clothing. "I believe that the profession of a translator is the humblest job this...woman could ever achieve." She thinks me to be a whore. "Where did you find her, the streets? Or did she come crawling into the palace asking for spare change and you took pity on her?"

Tension rises. I can see it in how the King now holds himself, shoulders tense, fists forming as his knuckles turn white, and as if a wave of annoyance rolls off him. It is as if the room darkens, the air no longer light, but like a weight upon my chest. "And you are judging yet another guest within the palace walls at just appearances. You should do a double take at yourself, Lady Ebony, especially at that pearl necklace around your neck and remind yourself that you gave yourself to a noble to earn those."

"My King, she is a whore-

"She is no whore, but a weary traveler that has a talent to offer me."

"What talent? She is probably going to rob you of your finest treasures-

A growl fills the air, shaking the walls and floor as my skin pales and I grab onto the chair for support, afraid of what this male is capable of. I may be playing with fire here that is more out of my control than I had anticipated. But the King seems to have a form of trust for me that is not common, something I can use to my advantage as well as a pray works out for me the best. "Know your place, Lady Ebony, for as much as you like that tongue of yours, I could easily cut it out."

That shuts her up for good.

"Now, Lady Ebony, did you have any intellectual commentary to add to this conversation that is worth interrupting my private hours for?" The King asks, now blocking my view of the woman of poise, his intimidating figure standing before me as I truly wonder what this man is capable of. He is a King, one with revenge strong in his blood for my father, a man that is not human, and eyes that tell me he is more than what he appears. He already appears to be a man of power and has proved himself to be so with that crown and the way he holds himself, but the way he growls, conducts himself, demands upmost respect from those under him, and the way others act around him, I know that I do not want to be around this male more than I must. But he is the way to find my father, how he has the best trackers working for him, the best warriors, those that know the lands of the realm more than I could ever. Staying beside the King is my best bet at finding my father, but I must also deceive this male more, to be able to escape his clutches as him and his men are led in the opposite direction of where my father is when I go to him.

The door shuts and I am informed that Lady Ebony has left the room, angered by the commentary of her tongue one day cut out of her mouth. One way to silence a woman who seems like her main power are the words she speaks with a silver tongue. "How much would it cost to hire you as a translator?" the King asks. "Paid in gold, silver, jewelry, or some other form of riches to you?" I have no money, no form of currency that this world uses. If I make my way and part with the King and his men, I will need money to pay for things, for food, shelter, and perhaps even a weapon to protect myself as I am simply a human in a world of the supernatural. "Recognition, fame?"

I shake my head, thinking of what I would need most. "Just gold coins will be enough, your majesty." He nods, crossing his arms as his eyes meet mine and once more I am pulled into a trance. The hairs on my arms raise, a gentle spark felt upon my upper left arm, right to where his fingers brush my skin, as if afraid to harm me. He barely touches me, as if I am made from glass, as if he is afraid I will break. Why? Is it some strange attraction? Perhaps he senses that I am not like the rest of the people who have passed through his palace, perhaps sensing a connection to my father and the man that killed his own father. That is all I can expect from this strange connection that this King seems to feel for me, a human in hiding. "Enough coins to make the journey back to my home after we have found this monster."

"Would you be willing to go home?" He asks, tilting his head to the side, and just as I rise to my feet to tell him that I would love to leave this palace for my home, I realize just how close we stand to one another, how our chests almost touch. His hand seems to levitate upwards, knuckles brushing my jawline, dancing across my skin as if feathers. "To leave this palace of marble halls and riches, of books dating back centuries holding so much of magic that scribes are not yet able to translate? There is work here within these walls that you would be praised for."

Finding myself surprised by this offer of a job, I still shake my head. "I am not one to be recognized for the work I have done here. I came to this palace for one reason only and once that justice is served, I will return to the pack that I call my family."

"To return to a society that probably does not recognize women as their equal?" He knows the society that I talk of better than I do because he is from here. I have no desire to go to those societies because I do not belong there, but I belong in a world of humans. I belong in a world where magic is just a trick that few preform and where science is what explains what I see every day. "You are a woman living in a reality that your society does not wish to represent. Here, within these walls of the palace, you could expand your knowledge, learn more than just simple laws and of magic, but help make those laws, see and even preform that magic, and be an equal to those around you."

His presence, his very essence, it seems to consume me, those eyes puling me and entangling me into his world as what he tells me, it would be appealing if I was who he believed me to be. "I require a simple life to keep my happy, nothing more or less. I will take what you pay me to return home and give me a safe journey there when this is all said and done. I will return home when I find what I have been looking for." Silence fills the small gap between us as the King keeps himself close to me and somehow, I do not move away. Could it be because I fear him lashing out if I move away? Could it be a sign of disrespect if I move away? "Now, when do we head out to this temple?"

Pulling away, the King takes in my appearance once more, the simple dress I wear, my hair undone, and a fear in my eyes cloaked by a feeling of ambition and excitement to leave this palace. "You are a unique woman, Candice," he whispers, voice softer than I have ever heard him speak, and as he turns to the door, he takes my arm, pulling me gently along with him as I use my free hand to pull my hair back and appear less of a prostitute. "I will have a maid send you a change of clothes for travel and get you a horse saddled up in the stables. After you change, head down to the stables and we will be ready to leave." That quick. It seems like I just arrive in this strange new world and now I am heading back to the mirror and temple where I had first arrived. As the King pulls me along with him down more stairs and halls, soon we come before a door painted lavender, women's voices behind as he lets go of my arm. "And, Candice, I will try everything I can to keep you here, to persuade you to stay within the palace walls," he states, looking right into my eyes as he says these words, this promise to me.

"Persuading me to stay within the walls of a palace that holds nothing I find valued to my heart, my King, that will not work," I reply, pulling away and turning the knob on the door as the King's eyes darker. "I shall see you at the stables."

I leave him in the hall as I enter the room and the lavender door shuts behind me as I take in a room filled with three maids packing up a golden trunk, shoving articles of clothing into the trunk. "My Lady," one of the women greet, and right away, as her bright green eyes meet mine and I spot the delicate, almost transparent, silver wings of hers, I know these women to not just be maids, but fairies. The size of perhaps a Hobbit, her blond hair is pulled back into a braided up-do, her smile wide, and holding out for me a simple dark purple dress for the ride ahead. "The King has informed us to pack you a trunk for two weeks, three pieces to be for celebrations or more elaborate dinners, seven for travel, and four for the purposes of more casual attire as you accompany the King and his guards." I nod, realizing just not the duration of time that I will be out on a horse and trying to find the man I know to be my father.

The fairy takes my hand, taking me past the other three fairies that look like her, right to a small changing area where she places the purple dress upon a hanger and helps me out of my dress, leaving me in a plane pair of bra and panties, confusing the fairy. I guess I am not in their typical form of undergarments. "These are...interesting," she comments, offering me a forced smile as she grabs me something similar to a night slip I would expect my mother to have worn thirty years ago. After the garment is on, next comes the dress, the dress falling over my head and onto my body, the sleeves fitting my arms well, golden embroidery on the ends, the front simple with a small slope to the top of my breasts, the back fully covered, a tad bit snug around my waist, and hitting the floor with a sense of elegance as a gold fabric belt with royal blue embroidery is along my waist.

Handing me a pair of brown riding boots, the fairy places them upon my feet, another working on my hair, braiding it back as I notice how quick this day has gone. One moment I am in the library and next thing I know the King has picked me up from the crowd, taken me to a balcony, held me over that balcony, I persuaded him to let me translate for him once we get to the temple where I arrived in this strange realm, and am now being dressed by fairies as warriors and the King and also getting ready for what seems like a long two weeks of travel. I have only ridden on a horse twice in my life, once at a camp where I learned that I could never be good at horseback riding, and a second time when my mother thought it would be a good bonding activity almost ten years ago.

"Are you ready to go, my Lady?" the same fairy asks, a gentle smile offered to me as I simply nod my head but know deep down that I am sure as hell not ready for what awaits me. I am scared, worried that the King will find out I may not be a werewolf unable to shift, but a human. Hell, if I am not careful, he will perhaps even uncover that I am Heka's daughter. Taking in a deep breath, I try and focus on the plan I have ahead, the plan that is changing with every event that has occurred. I need to be prepared for the worst, I need to know what to do if things do not go my way, because if I am not, I could be murdered just as these people plan to do to my father if they find him. "The King does not take too lightly to those who are late in his presence."

I need to do what I can to keep the King under control and trust me more than his best warriors. "I am ready."

The fairy nods, opening the lavender door for me as we once more travel down the hallway, the long, white marble floor stretched before us as royal blue swirls can be seen in the floor, like crystals in the marble, reminding me of an ocean with the vibrant shades of blue. The walls are white with gold patterns, the windows stretching high, displaying the marble buildings beyond the palace and to the capital as the snow still falls upon the ground. It is moments and views like this that I am in full awe of this realm, of the magic that seems to keep this world alive and unique. Compared to the world I was raised in, this is what I would like to think magic capable of, of creating lands of beauty and as if created by a god or goddess talented in the arts. This world is filled of so much beauty, yet I know that a darkness is also part of this land, a darkness that I have yet to discover.

As we take staircase after staircase leading down, soon enough I hear the sound of horses, of metal banging against metal, voices shouting, and commotion. It is a tight schedule after all. Taking in a deep breath to help calm my nerves, soon enough I am surrounded by massive men, tall, muscular, dressed in crimson red and silver, three carrying the palace flag on poles as they mount their black horses. Those dressed more importantly with embroidery on their armor, they ride upon black horses, each horse with their tail braided, what looks like beads woven into the hairs. The beads have engravings on them, engravings that seem to glow with shades of silver or gold, symbolizing something I am not yet aware of. And in the middle of men shouting orders, tossing around swords to others, handing others long and deadly arrows, and running around, in the eye of the storm stand their King, his royal robes replaced with a simple black fur cloak that falls to his ankles, the hood of the cloak down as it spreads across his shoulders, the inside of the cloak a crimson material from silk. Dressed for a long journey, his boots are warm-looking, black pants tucked in, a leather sash going across his chest, stretching from his left shoulder to his waist as I see knives stored there, a compass, a few beads like his more important warriors, and what looks to be a small glass bottle filled with a type of gray sand.

His eyes meet mine, a swirl of purple, blue, silver, and black, his eyes dilating, hand reaching up to run his fingers through his dark locks. You can tell he is the man of importance out of this group. As a warrior walks before the line of gaze we hold, a weight is places upon my shoulders, my reflexes quick as I turn around to see the fairy placing a cloak just like the King's on me, but this one is the fur of what a fox would have, a mix of red and brown, warming me up instantly as the stable doors are pulled open and the cold air enters.

Looking back to where the King stood, he is gone, the eye of the storm having moved as I hear his voice, stern and sharp, command-ing someone to grab someone a horse. As I try and find where he has gone, I meet a pair of gray eyes, a man holding their reins of a gray horse. "Lady Candice, your horse as promised by the King Kyril."

Kyril. So that is the name of the man that wishes to murder my father, the man who has hired me to become his translator. It suits him.

"Do you require help, my lady, to mount your horse?" the warrior asks, seeing that I have not yet climbed onto the horse as it seems like everyone else is doing so.

"No thank you, I've got it," I inform, hoping I still have the upper body strength that I once did when I did gymnastics years ago. Taking the handle of the saddle, I pull myself up, swinging my left leg over as I realize that I have just mounted the horse no lady should. Quickly I fix my mistake, my legs on the same side as I remember an old scene from a childhood movie of a princess learning how to rise a horse. I may not have a fake leg to fake how I am sitting and get away with my legs on either side of the horse, but I do know that this is very uncomfortable. After looking around, I realize a very common component of this group set out to the temple: I am the only female on this journey.

Just as I look to the gates of the stable and how more men are outside the stable walls, on their horses as they wait for everyone inside this one, a midnight black horse pulls up beside me, the eyes of the horse pitch black, the reins of the horse an obsidian color, and the man upon the horse is the one that has offered me a job back in the palace when this journey is done. Little does he know I will be gone the moment I know where to find my father. "You look a little uncomfortable, Lady Candice, have you ever ridden a horse before?" He points out, but it not that which makes me raise an eyebrow, but the fact that he has just placed the term lady before my name unlike before when he would just say my name.

"Just not familiar with them," I reply, looking back to the outside, the snow falling still. Kyril nods, pulling forward to meet my gaze once more, pulling his hood on as the chilly air only gets closer to reaching the main source. I follow his moves, pulling my hood on as the warmth surround me.

Kyril nods, trotting his horse to stand before mine, facing me as his men exit the stable, soon enough just leaving the two of us and a couple of others alone in the stable. "My King, I do believe that these men are waiting on us to begin the ride," I point out as the warriors await us outside, to begin our ride.

"Remember that promise I made to you, Candice?" He asks, using my name with no title before it as only a few stable boys are around us.

"I do, how you will try and persuade me to take a job within the palace walls," I reply, hoping he will leave it at that and nothing more.

Kyril allows for a smirk to pull at his lips. "Consider is more than a job of a translator, but also a companion to your King." And just like that, he pulls the reins of his horse away, the horse trotting out to the warriors awaiting as I stand frozen in the stables, understanding now that it will take a lot more than just his trust to win over to get out of here. A lot more than I would like to ever have to deal with. Taking in a deep breath, I leave the stable with my horse, only for a warrior to come up to me, leading me to the front to where the King awaits me, a sly smile upon his face as we set off into the winter cold.

Chapter 10

As the moon rises into the night, the stars also come out, the chill of the night settling into the camp that was just set up two hours ago. With voices filling the night, songs of old stories from years ago, and tents set up for the stay tonight, for the past couple of hours I have stayed within the warmth of my tent. The small tent is more luxurious than I would have expected, more than just a simple tent pitched with enough room for a small cot. Inside the tent is massive, the floor covered in a rather large rug, woven together by the threads as it creates a pattern of deer being hunted. My so-called cot is rather a comfy mattress, a white fur blanket used to keep me warm while I sleep, tapestries upon the walls of the tent to keep me warm inside, and the chest that the fairies packed for me is pushed up against once of the walls. Luxurious camping for sure even if for one night. All of this for one night, the same men that set up this tent house to take it down and then set it up day after day.

"Lady Candice," a voice announces, greeting me as the individual enters my tent, pushing through the front flaps, greeting me with a small smile. Dressed in a brown fur cloak, crimson uniform, striking silver eyes, and light blond hair, this male is a stranger to me, a stranger that is tall just like the King, and just as intimidating as any of the warriors outside. "Allow me to introduce myself, my Lady, for I am Duke Gravon of the Eastern Islands. My King has told me that you are the translator."

"The King has informed your correctly," I respond, welcoming the male into my tent, his kinder face making me feel more at ease with him than any of the men in this camp. "What can I do for you?"

Gravon takes a seat on the chest the fairies packed, the metallic trunk perfect for sitting on as he uses it to its full advantage. "My Lady, I have been on several of these quests for the King. I never doubt his determination to find this retched male that murdered the past King like a monster, but this is to be my sixth quest and every time these result in dead ends. This man that we are hunting, he is far superior. The fox that cannot be caught." If what he says is true, these two weeks that we are set out for, they could end with no more leads and I will have wasted my time here. I am on a schedule to find my father, yet I do not even have a schedule made. All my life I have been organized, always having a schedule that I stick to, and now here I am, millions of loose ends and paths I could take as I have no idea where any one leads. "What makes you think that by having you, and I mean no offense to your talents as a translator here, do you think that we can actually find a major lead on our prey?"

Do I tell this man that there is a book left at the Temple that could give me clues? It would be way to suspicious, as these men would expect me to have never visited this Temple, much less know of a random journal to be there. Gravon does not like the fact that my father is hard to even trace his tracks. One of his many hidden talents, my father could cover up his tracks, disappear into thin air. He was a magician after all, someone who would vanish before your very eyes, giving the audience no idea where he could be. He made a profession off this, meaning that these warriors and Lords are hunting a man trained to erase himself from the world. "If this Temple holds what I hope, and believe it will, Duke Gravon, then we will have a starting point that you and your men could have dreamed of ages ago. I was taught by this wretched man himself as a child, his language and even some of his tricks, but he turned on my pack, slaughtering my mother as well as others I held close to my heart."

"And so, the student is to help strike down her teacher, very poetic," Duke Gravon comments to my explanation of why he should put his trust in me. Rising to his feet, the Duke bows his head to me, offering me yet again a friendly smile. "Well then, Lady Candice, if the King has decided to trust you in this hunt, then he is wise and no fool. I must go now, to converse with the other nobles. Good night, Lady Candice, and may the gods bring you dreams of great joy."

There are certain things within the world I come from that I have lost in the fire that is Iduna and the whole drama with my father. Well, not exactly fire, but the mess that occurred from his parting with his family, career, and the very reality he lived in. Did my father not find life with a woman that loves him and a daughter that looked up to him enough? My father was lost in that fire years ago, but as I stare at the ceiling of my tent, the winds blowing fierce outside, my mind rushes through the faces of those that I left behind what feels like ages ago. I had many close friends, even a boyfriend that had grown distant weeks before I graduated high school. It is if I cannot even make out his face even more, my mind has barely even crossed the thought of him since I found the key and unlocked this world of crazy magic. His name? I know that much. His name is Nicholas, a light blond with striking green eyes, one of the few boys to never tease me about my father's so-called death, and someone who faded away when we discovered we would be heading to separate universities. To think he has hardly crossed my mind leaves me at a loss for words, unable to process that a boy that once took up so much of my mind has become almost a forgotten memory. But Nicholas is not something that keeps me up tonight, listening to the raging winds and the chatter of the warriors, but rather the woman I left behind in her already accepted solitude. My mother had been living in her own little reality for quite some time before I entered this realm, even about to fly out for a matter of weeks, telling me of her plans the day that I left her.

My mother used to show up to my childhood events, school plays, and small parties, but she never intended to make them really. She would mark them down on her calendar to make the young version of me happy, telling me that she would be home from her travels to make it. The most she ever attended in a year was three, making that fifth-grade year of mine one that I would always remember unlike the rest where she would forget, be gone, or too tired to attend. My own mother is the reason for when I think of my future self as a mother, to do everything exactly opposite of her. My mother is the reason for why having children of my own makes me scared of raising them like she did me. But then again, my husband will not be some magician that is world-famous and leaves one day for a world he believed existed outside of our own.

"Lady Candice?"

I perk up, posture straight, eyes trained on the entrance to my tent, quickly pulling my hair back into a bun. Why am I nervous? That is the voice of the man who has hired me, and as the man whose voice just called out for me enters my tent, I begin to wonder if these people ever ask for permission to enter a lady's tent. "My King," I greet in return, rising to my feet as I bow my head quickly, hoping for a short conversation compared to one like before when he held me over a fall that would result in my death. "I am afraid I was not expecting a visit from you tonight."

King Kyril nods, a small smile spreading across his face as he looks around my tent, to the tapestries hung on the walls to keep the tent insulated. The tapestries hold patterns of flowers, rivers, forests, and moons as wolves run through the forest. "I am sorry to bother you at this hour, my Lady, but I was unable to sleep and saw your tent was still lit and decided to pay you a visit." Rather than the Duke that was here earlier, King Kyril does not sit on my trunk, but right on my bed, right where I was just laying down. Just because he hired me does not mean he has the right to be inviting himself into my tent and sitting where I sleep.

"I was just going to sleep," I inform, crossing my arms as I stand before the King, tired and worn out from hours of riding a horse through the chilling winter weather. The King nods, knowing full well that my past statement was a passive-aggressive way to tell him to leave, yet he stays put, admiring the tapestries around my tent.

"Trying to sleep with the noise outside is hardly possible, Candice," Kyril comments, using no formal title as he meets my eyes, eyes an electric blue with a mix of silver. I would love to ask him why the color of his eyes change so much, why they swirl with color and can darken in a matter of seconds. "And seeing that most of my men are drinking to the night and I wanted to remain sober, I have come to pay you a visit."

I force a smile onto my face. "You are so kind." My voice is flat and monotone, seeing a smirk pull at the King's lips. "But I really was trying to sleep, King Kyril-

"You can drop the title in private, Candice," the King informs, cutting me off as he rises to his feet, towering over me. My throat runs dry and I find myself raising an eyebrow as he practically orders me to drop his title when it is just the two of us. "It puts a barrier between us that I am not fond of."

I tilt my head to the side, telling myself to stand my ground here. "We are business partners here, my King, and that means we stick to formal titles as our relationship is one of formality," I state, voice sharp, and as I watch his darkening eyes, I know I have made a mistake.

Just as I take a small step back, to place some sort of distance between the two of us, the King takes a large stride forward, imposing upon my personal space as his scent consumes me and I am cast under that strange spell of his that seems to reel me in. My breathing gets heavier as he raises his hand, knuckles brushing over my cheek as he holds me in his intense stare, as if keeping my body frozen in place. "Tell me, dearest little Candice, do you not feel the pull between the two of us? The dance our souls are begging us to partake in. The temptations of the mind and body that pull us closer every moment?" My chest becomes heavy, shoulders feeling like a weight has been placed upon them. His hands move to the back of my neck, gently cupping it as my eyes grow wide. "So delicate, so small, so beautiful. The gods crafted you in their very hands unlike anyone else I have ever met."

My hair comes out of its bun, the King's fingers pulling the hair tie out as my hair falls down my back, the locks long and silky. Fingers run through my hair, touching it as if some delicacy never felt before. Eyes locked with mine, he moves in closer, hands settling on my hips as I feel sparks run through my body, shivers running along my spin as the King's eyes search my face, as if memorizing every feature.

"And I am afraid, my King," I begin, falling out of his trance as I take a step back, placing a good stance between us, "that you are stepping out of your boundaries here. I am here to be your translator and nothing more."

Taking the cloak I wore on the ride, I pull it over my body, heading for the tent entrance, the King calling out my name softly as I enter the chilling wind of the night. As I pull my hair back up and venture out to the boarder of the camp, the hill we are placed upon giving me a view of the wildness ahead. Mountains lay beyond the forest ahead; the darkness of the night already having settled in as the moon lights the outlines of the forest and mountains. Tomorrow we will journey out that way, many of the men having discussed the snow that will act as a dangerous challenge for our horses. Looking over my shoulder to see the entrance of my tent, the King stands there, figure outlined in black, watching me from afar as he looks tense. He is not happy with me, but I do not give a damn. I do not wish to wind up beside a man that is trying to kill my father and that is not even human. I am here to find my father, not let some sort of lust get in the way of that and only make me dig my grave deeper than it has become. The King wants something from me I will never offer him. We are business partners, and sure, that may be strange to him because of my gender, but he will learn from me to not underestimate a woman.

When I was told by my mother about sex when I was seventeen (after I had learned about the birds and the bees several years prior), she told me that before she met my father, she was in a rough place. The daughter of a single mother who could never give up her lazy lifestyle to pay for my mother and her little sister, my mother became a dancer, working the nights to pay for her sister as well as her college education. She met my dad when he was looking for an assistant, traveling through Europe where she just so happened to be on a study abroad program. He saw her drunk at a pup, dancing on one of the tables, drinking away the news of her mother having died due to an overdose. He carried her back to her temporary residence in that city, making sure she was safe, and when she woke up with a miserable hangover, he offered her the role of his assistant. Not the most romantic, but it taught me about my mother, about how she was brought up and what she did to make a living. No, this part of my life is nothing like that part of her story, but it reminds me that I need to do what I can to find my father. No, I will not go and jump the King's bones, but I will try and keep up a friendly relationship with him. I need his trust and nothing more, just that trust to get what I need from the Temple and from the trace of my father. In the end, I will lead him and his men in the opposite direction of my father as I go to my father, but to reach the light at the end of the tunnel, I will need aid.

Taking in a deep breath, I look back to the mountains in the distance, where Soka found me and took me to her village. In those mountains is the temple where I hope to find some answers and win the trust of those I will betray. But why did my father kill the past King? It is his own fault that these men are after him, yet why did he kill him? I never knew that my father had a violent bone in his body, the guts to kill someone, and now, he is in hiding so something. Wouldn't he have come back after so many years here, have completed whatever he was wanting to do here by now...or did he never intend on coming back home to his wife and daughter?

"Damn you, dad," I whisper, fists clenched as I storm back to my tent, the King gone as I know I can sleep soundly now. Blowing out the candles, the darkness fills the room as I lie back down in my temporary bed, the covers pulled over my frame as I close my eyes.

Morning comes fast, the horses mounted quickly after camp was taken down in a matter of minutes. Four warriors had taken down my tent faster than I could have ever predicted, telling me that they hoped I had a good night's sleep. Did I? After some stirring and restlessness, I was able to go into a deep sleep, only to wake up to a horn blowing, informing everyone we would head out in an hour. Dressing myself was a challenge as I had to lace up the back of my dress today on my own, the new dress upon my figure different than before as this one was made from a dark green material, golden embroidery, and a dip in the front that makes me scared of bending over too far. With my hair braided back, the same fox-fur cloak as yesterday draped over my shoulders, and a new layer of snow having landed on the ground, I am glad to hand my feet not on the ground, but elevated as I sit on my horse. Everyone is loaded up, just waiting for King Kyril who has yet to get onto his horse, chatting with some warrior who holds a flag for his kingdom.

I can tell today's ride will be one of few words spoken between the King and I, the atmosphere to be tense due to the events and words spoken last night. As the King walks over to his horse, his eyes meet mine, a cold stare meeting my soft gaze as his horse's hooves dig into the snow. "Let us ride for the mountains," he announces to the warriors, eyes still glued to mine as we take off, the horses ready for the day ahead as I simply pull my cloak closer and try to take my mind off last night's conversation.

Five hours later and we have stopped for a quick lunch, a simple meal of some chicken-like animal with a weird sounding name and bread. I sit beside my horse, away from the small collective groups of those brought along for the hunt of Heka, conversing and laughing as I keep to myself. The only female on the journey makes me feel out of place, afraid being surrounded by so many intimidating men in a land I have no idea where to flee to. I just wish to keep to myself for the two weeks I may be out here, to be boring and an introvert. But that will not be the most successful plan with a King who lusts after you and has been turned down.

"Tell me, Candice, do you not enjoy the view?" Speak of the devil. Looking up from my food, I meet the eyes of a man who is used to getting whatever he wants. He looks to the North, to where the snow-covered mountains are, a breathtaking view for sure. "Or is a slice of stale bread more entertaining?"

I look back to my bread, petting the front legs of my horse as it stands by the stone I have placed myself upon. "I just want to get to the mountains before nightfall."

Rising to my feet, I finish off my bread, knowing that with a full mouth that the King can expect no immediate answer or comment from anything he may say or ask while I chew. Rather than speak, he waits for me, hands behind his back as I decide to chew my food slower than ever before. He waits, eyes glued to the side of my face the entire time as I stare at the mountains ahead. "You must not have been popular with the elders of your pack," the King comments, crossing his arms. "Your way of thinking, to speak to your

King the way you have dared, to call us business partners, to even mock me."

I raise an eyebrow, swallowing the food as I have stalled long enough. "I guess I owe my extraordinary way of thinking to the devil himself, the great and damned Heka."

What have I done...

My arm is grabbed, the King taking care of business himself as I expected him to order one of his guards to take me from his presence. Rather than head for one of the horses or for some sword to behead me, the King pulls me into the forest that surrounds us, off the trail we stopped on. Deeper into the forest we go as I tell myself to keep my mouth shut and not anger the supernatural being who drags me out of sight of the group we travel with. As King Kyril comes to a stop, we are in a small clearing where the trees surround us, the King standing in front of me as his eyes are pitch black. "If you didn't mean so much to me already I would not have hesitated to chop off that pretty head of yours in front of all of my men." My skin pales as the King places his hands on my frail shoulders, fingers lightly digging into my skin as he tilts his head to the side. "If you were not so important to me, I would have cut off that tongue of yours the day we met."

"And why didn't you? Why do I mean so much to you the moment we met?" I ask, my voice shaky as I try and hold my head high. "Why didn't you take that precious knife of yours and slice my tongue off like you would have anyone else? After all, we are not equals now, are we? You are above me due to some absurd social class."

My back meets the bark of a tree, his hands on my throat, fingers wrapped around as they apply minimal pressure. Conflict. Conflict is all I see in his eyes as they seem to redden. "You have no idea how dead you would be right now if you were not the woman of the soul that my soul was destined to dance with."

What does that mean? I am some soul mate, because that is what he is making it out to be?

"It is because you have not shifted yet into your wolf that you cannot feel what I feel for you. That pull, that electric and magnetic pull that sends sparks through my body every time we touch. That magical spell you seem to cast me under whenever you look at me. You are the most beautiful woman I have ever looked at and it makes me want to rip the heavens apart because you cannot feel these things." He seems to come closer, lips dangerously close to mine as he has no idea that I have felt everything he has just described. "Even now, with my hands around your neck, if I didn't feel the sparks, you would fall limp."

"That's a great thought to have in my head," I mumble, not liking one bit who he talks about violent acts at me.

"I do not want to watch you go back to your pack when we are done here because I cannot stand to not be around you. I would declare war on the gods and rip through the caverns of hell to keep you by my side for eternity."

"I have a life outside of yours," I whisper, noticing how much closer the King has come now, nose brushing mine as I try and remain calm. Try and remain calm as he tells me he would do anything to keep me in his presence while all I can think about is the fact that I will need to leave him very soon. "I have a pack, a home, and friends."

Kyril looks to me, eyes swirling with a dark violet color, hands upon my neck, his body tense as I wonder what is running through that mind of his. He says he will not harm me, but at this moment, as his hands are wrapped around my neck, I do not fully trust his words. It is like the hold a boa constrictor has its prey in, tight and secure, the prey in its mercy as it knows it cannot break free. Even if I put up a fight, he would overpower me, for I am a mere mouse compared to his snake-like grip, easy to catch and kill. With my back pressed against the tree and the bark digging into my back, I decide enough is enough, testing my limits.

"No," I inform, voice stern as his midnight blue eyes meet mine, lips slightly parted as his breathing is heavy. "No, this cannot happen. I have a family to return to, people that I love, a pack that has plans for me in my years to come." The King releases me, watching as I collect myself, my head high and shoulders rolled back. "You are my King and nothing more."

"You have no idea how wrong you are. You can feel some of those same effects, the sparks, the attraction. You are lying to me, to yourself, for your future belongs with me and not with those from your pack!" Kyril argues, hands cupping my face as he holds me close. "We belong together, and I will prove that to you."

I shake my head. "My mind is already made up, it was made up before we even met, my King, and when we are done here, I will return home."

He shakes his head, pulling my face close, lips pressed upon my forehead as my hands reach up, holding onto his strong arms. "And I will make sure you can never return home."

Chapter 11

As the day comes to an end and I find myself standing before my tent being set up for the night, the placement of the King's tent has changed tonight. No longer is that massive gold and crimson tent pitched beside his lead warrior's, but beside his tracker and the very women he swore he would never allow to return home. Crossing my arms, I watch as the four men pitch my tent, a horse standing beside me with a cart containing the other objects in my tent like my chest and cot. As I look to my right, I see the King's men setting up his tent, identical to mine in shape, but twice the size of mine which is already big compared to the tents that the warriors share with multiple individuals. The King is walks towards his tent as I take a seat upon one of the rocks by the horse I am by, hands on my knees as I find my eyelids heavy. I just want a good night's sleep, to dream of nothing but going home and laying back in my own bed. Usually for nights like this where I find myself tired and having to stay up for a few more minutes, I would pull out my phone and play some game, but out here, in Iduna, it would be unrealistic to even have the technology of a Nokia phone.

"Lady Candice, getting set up for the night?" The King asks me, one of the few questions he has asked me since that incident in the woods where I found myself against a tree and being told he would never let me return home. He thinks my home to be some simple pack of wolves a month's travel away, but little does he know it is in another realm and tomorrow, perhaps all I need to do is say the right words and slip back into the mirror. Would I go back home tomorrow if I had enough of this world and gave up on my father? A small piece of me dares me to go back home, to forget about my father here, to go back to my home and greet those that I love with a smile as I have missed them. But I need to find my father, to know why he left years ago, to know why he killed a King, and to know why he never came back home. "Would you like to have a drink in my tent when it is done being pitched for the night?" It is asked as any question would be asked, but I know it is more of a demand than anything.

A demand I will not submit to. "I would, but perhaps another night. I am afraid I am lightheaded and need all the rest I can attain tonight," I reply kindly, looking back to the tent being pitched before me as I nervously tap my fingers along to some old 90's tune. Rather than leave it be like I had hoped Kyril would, he walks over to me, crouching down for his eyes to meet mine as I can see his jaw is clenched, lips slightly parted as he is about to answer, but stops himself.

"You sure you do not need a drink? Something strong to cure that headache of yours?" He asks, making it clear to me that he will not back down from me going into his tent and having some conversation and drink with him. I cannot win here, seeing that he is stubborn. I remind myself that soon I will leave him, that I will find my exit and take it the first chance that I get.

Taking in a deep breath, I reluctantly nod my head. "Just one and nothing more. I need my sleep," I strong state, making sure he understands that I will not put up with him past that amount of time I will give him. As his tent is fully pitched and his men begin to unload the massive amount of crap he packed with him, he reminds me of my mother for a journey. How much stuff he has brought with him reminds me of her, how she over packs for every single trip, three suitcases for a weekend getaway. Looking back to the King who stands up back to his original height, I ask myself what will happen if the Temple holds nothing for me to be useful for and he decides to call the trip off and pulls me back with him to his palace. I am certain that the journal is within the walls of that Temple, but what if something happened and it is not there? My whole cause for going along on this trip will be gone and the King will make sure I never leave him. I should not concern myself with those thoughts before bed when I want a peaceful sleep but knowing that I must converse with the King first guarantees a stressful night.

"Lady Candice," he calls out, holding out his hand to me as I see that in the time my thoughts consumed me, the men have finished unloading and his royal tent is all ready for the night. I do not take his hand, rather getting onto my own two feet without any assistance as I keep my eyes trained on the tent and not the King who gives me a stern glare. Walking ahead of him, I enter the tent first, the ostentatious interior of the tent informing me that he does indeed like to travel in style. A cot that is more of a kind-sized bed than cot is placed in the center, a dark brown fur blanket with golden embroidery on the edges covering the bed with two silky pillows, two wooden nightstands on either side of the bed holding candles lit as well as a fancy bow with four arrows. All along the walls are extravagant tapestries of mountains and oceans, four trunks on one side with a King's armor placed upon one, a harp-like instrument on another, and the third opened to where cloaks made of expensive fur is on display. For the other side of the tent, bookshelves with ancient-looking and homemade books and journals as well as liquor to the max. "Take a seat," King Kyril adds to the silence of the night, motioning me towards a small sitting area right before the foot of the bed, comfy looking as I want to just lie there and sleep.

I do not upset the King, taking a seat on one of the chairs, hands clasped together as I find myself nervous in his tent. Am I afraid of him taking advantage of me, forcing me into something I do not wish to do? For some reason, I trust him, I believe that he will do nothing to force me into anything. I have no idea where this trust has come from, but I am not a fan of it. "What do you prefer to drink?"

"Water," I reply, finding myself craving the tasteless substance as I just want to have that in my system and no alcohol.

"I doubt water is what you need for that headache of yours," Kyril comments, going to his shelf of liquor as he takes out a fancy glass and pours me some lavender-colored drink. "I think you'll take a liking in this one." I have had many alcoholic drinks due to cliché high school parties and have come to know my liquor names well, but I have no idea what this is or how my body will react to it. Never take drinks from strangers, but right now, I have not too much of a choice due to my weird trusting him. "Drink." Handing me the glass, I thank the King, looking to the liquid inside as it smells like what I would expect a bachelorette party to smell like. As the King pours the same drink for himself, he walks back over to me, sitting across from me as he raises his glass, toasting. "To a successful day tomorrow," he toasts, watching as I raise my glass as well.

"To a successful day tomorrow," I reply, cheering with him as we both take a drink, the taste of the liquid filling my mouth as it is like a bitter cinnamon with rum. It is good to say the least. A good flavor for alcohol.

Within ten minutes our drinks are down, the two of us more relaxed as I find that I am no longer lightheaded. With barely any words spoken between the two of us, I decide to make the move, knowing that I just want to curl up on my cot and sleep. "Well, my King, thank you for the drink, but I am off to bed now."

The King's eyebrows knit together, his lips forming a thin line as he shakes his head. "Even if I order it, you still have the guts to call me your King rather than my own name."

He's back on this again. "I find it unnecessary seeing that I am simply someone you have hired to track this human."

Silence. Something is off. The King raises an eyebrow at me, not looking mad or annoyed, but shocked, a questioning look crossing his face as he tilts his head to the side. Getting to his feet, the King clasps his hands behind his back, looking down to me as he can't seem to understand something. "You studied under this man, correct?" he asks as I nod for my reply. "Did he teach you the ways of his people? Anything else about some Pressendent that ruled his land?"

"President," I correct, wondering how he know about the title of President. Did my father try and teach Kyril about the human realm? "He said that his ruler was elected by the people. He said that the President once came to him to see magic." I need to seem like I have a small idea about the government of my country. "Why does this concern you?" I ask, rising to my feet as the King bites his lip, heading for the books he brought with him.

The King seems to be onto something. I have no idea if I should be worried for my cover here as a werewolf. "You see, Heka, when he came to the palace for the first time, he told my father of a realm that he came from, saying that it was one beyond our own realm's years. He told us about these carriages that used no horses, about ships that sailed in the sky, and of his race. He said that they called what he did magic because they had no other word for it. Spells, potions, and powers were fictional in his world. My father allowed Heka to teach me things of his world, and being just a child then, I was obsessed with the way he realm worked, wanting to go there one day, but he told me that his realm was filled with monsters of the darkness." My father said that? Monsters of the darkness? I find that hard to believe seeing that the supernatural are just some strange belief that people have back home, but then again, my reality has been flipped upside down ever since I discovered another realm outside my own. "What did he tell you of his home?"

This is where I choose my words wisely, where I decide where there is too much information and where there is too little. "It was so longer ago that I met him," I begin, trying to make him understand that I would not know too much because it was supposedly years ago that Heka came to my village and killed my made-up mother. "He talked of many things, of states that were many feet high and buildings that seemed to reach the clouds. He described his home as something beyond what the gods could create, of lakes made by man, of a source of light that never seemed to run out, and of boxes that showed stories."

The King nods, grabbing more of the drink as he offers me some more as well. Nodding my head, he pours me another glass of the unknown substance, telling me that his father was in awe of Heka, that his father thought of Heka as some demigod. To think my father was seen as this to the man he would later slay. "My father trusted that monster...in the end his trust landed him with three arrows in his chest and my mother went insane. I was just a child then, a child who saw his teacher slaughter his father and drive his mother insane until her long anticipated death. Mother was kept an eye on every second, my father's elders afraid of her taking her own life." Is my father the bad guy? "She was on her death bed when she took my hand and told me she wished Heka had struck her down, so she would not wake up every day without her soulmate by her side. She said Heka made life become a bitter taste in her mouth that you just want to spit out."

I cannot let his testimony destroy what I have always thought of my father to be, but, I have only known my father from few memories, what my mother would say of him, and what the media would portray him as. In my memories, he loved me and would give me the world if I asked, to my mother, he was the man she fell head over heels for and gave her a life worth living, and for the media, my father was a man who was always mysterious, his private life unknown, but he know how to make women swoon and elites appraise him. But hearing this, hearing how my father supposedly destroyed this King's family and life, it is like I did not know my father at all.

"That man was born with a silver tongue," Kyril adds to the silent, taking a swing at his drink as I stare at my own, as if having lost my urge for the alcohol. "Who knows how many other lives he has ruined with his toxic presence. He has ruined both of ours."

"Yes, he has," I mumble, deciding to chug the rest of my drink as I recall all the nights I watched my mother sit in my father's side of their closet, holding onto old shirts of his, trying to see if they still held the scent of him. I recall nights where I would walk past her door, hearing her cries in the dark as she called out his name. Some nights were filled with her sorrow as she could only sob...other nights were fueled by fire. I remember walking into the house on the day they would have celebrated their twenties wedding anniversary, my mother screaming profundities of my father as she threw old magazines with his face pastured over them into the lit fireplace. She hurled some of his works into the fire, works from some water cage, all his notes consumed in the flames. Her wedding dress even became part of the ash.

"He ruined my mother," I whisper, finding my eyes watering as I just want to forget the night my mother took a gun to her head and told me she wanted to do it so badly, that she was a coward because she could never pull the trigger. I had told her she had me in her life to live for... but she just smiled and shook her head. "My mother was a hardworking and sweet before Heka took her from me." I take in a shaky breath as the King takes a seat at the foot of his bed. "She fell for him, and in the end, he ripped her heart out and I just sat and watched like a fool." It is true, what happened, but my words are not literal. "He was like a father to me and now he is just a man whose demons are out to play."

A hand lands on my shoulder, gently rubbing it as I lean into the odd warmth and sparks, closing my eyes as I try and keep the tears in. Taking in a deep breath, I open my eyes and rise to my feet, setting the glass upon one of the small tables. "Thank you for the drink and the conversation, my King, but it is time I called it a night," I inform, bowing my head as the King shakes his head, pinching the bridge of his nose.

"I have never told anyone about my mother, Candice, about her final words to me." My eyes meet his watery eyes, the once vibrant colors now dull as they do not even swirl. "About how she wanted to die with my father years ago. Heka destroyed the family I loved, and I will bring him to justice."

With his words, I leave.

Morning could not arrive sooner as I wake up to find the camp bursting with noise as the sun rises. Rolling onto my back, the cot beneath me is stiff, a small headache occurring as I recall the night before. After Kyril told me he would bring my father to justice, I came back and stared at the ceiling, recalling every memory I could about the man that raised me. About the man that took from my mother that happiness she had always deserved. About the man who took from me a childhood worth remembering as the memories that should be happy only leave a sour taste in my mouth and I want to call him a greedy bastard that only cared about what his magic could achieve rather than his own damn family. What was his plan in the end when this is all said and done? Does my father even have a goal here that once it is obtained, he would come home, because it has taken him many years. You would think he would have come back home into the arms of the woman who loves him and the daughter he never got to raise. Did he ever want to go back home? Mother knew what he was doing, that he was going into some place she had no idea what it was, but did she know what he would be doing here? The journal holds so much of what I must ask. The journal that I will hopefully be able to find today. I learned just this morning that it will be a mile hike to the temple, the horses cannot handle the steep and narrow pathway to the Temple.

Grabbing my clothes for the day, I change quick, trying to ignore the headache that is currently making me want to bang my head against someone's metal armor. Already for the day, I take in a deep breath, throwing my cloak over my shoulders as I exit my tent and welcome in the pale morning sky. It's colder today, the mountains having no mercy for the souls passing through them. Snow covers the ground as my boots sink into it, my fingers numb as Duke Gravon comes up to me, offering me a friendly smile as he does so. "My dear Lady Candice, are you ready for the adventure ahead?"

Looking to the path we will hike towards the Temple, I think of the cold weather ahead, of the possible things that the journal could hold. "I do hope so," I reply, looking over the Duke's shoulder to see King Kyril exiting his tent, shouting orders to a few of his trackers, telling them to be ready to leave within the next ten minutes.

"You carry no weapon on you, my Lady, do you not expect an attack?"

"An attack? From whom?" I ask, raising an eyebrow as the Duke causes worry to fuel my headache. When I arrived here, Soka was the one to greet me and no one else. I never saw any signs of threat except for the storm she was worried about. Is there a possibility of an attack?

Holding out a small object wrapped in leather, the Duke smiles to me, telling me he hopes we find a trace of the prey, and he walks off, leaving me with his small gift. I unwrap the object, the hold handles of a dagger falling into my hand as the blade runs sharp and thin, ready to sink into the flesh of any threat. It is a beautiful dagger, the weapon light, the handle carved with many engravings of some type of Hieroglyphics. This is weird. I have been able to read every form of language present in Iduna and yet this writing system I cannot read. My palms become sweaty as I worry that I may have overestimated how well I have been naturally able to read this realm's language. Is it from Iduna? It looks incredibly similar to Egyptian Hieroglyphics, but it cannot be. These people know nothing of my world, and if they do, only what my father has told them. My father's stage name is the Egyptian word for magic, but I highly doubt it that he brought a dagger with him and Duke Gravon got hold of it. But that is the only reasonable way I can think of me not being able to read the language.

"Candice, how did you sleep?" a familiar voice asks, causing me to jump as it tugs me away from my thoughts. Turning around, I greet the familiar pair of eyes that are always changing, the events from last night replaying in my head as he opened to me, and in return, I did as well, realizing the toxicity that my father placed in my life when he drew himself from it.

I lie. "Very well." Looking back to the passage through the mountains that we will be taking, my toes already numb as I worry that I will get frostbite. "But cold," I add, looking back to the King to find him staring at the dagger from Duke Gravon.

n"Do you plan on just holding that or putting it somewhere?" He asks, referring to the weapon as I open my cloak, looking at the inside lining to where I found a small pocket the other day. Wrapping it back up in the leather casing, I slide it into the small pouch of my cloak, looking back to the King as he simply holds out his gloved hand, a small glass bottle in his palm filled with a small silver substance. "A small potion to get rid of the cold. I know because you can't shift yet that you have no wolf to help warm you up." I nod, thanking the King as I take the small bottle, barely the size of my pinkie finger as I down the sweet-tasting liquid. Instantly I feel warmer, my toes regaining their sense of touch as I see the warriors and trackers are ready to head out, all loaded up for the small hike.

"Let us go."

Within the first five minutes of the hike, the camp has faded away in the mist of the mountains, snow still falling as we march through a small cavern where icy rocks line the walls. All warmed up from the King's potion, I find the cloak I wear unnecessary, wanting to throw it into the snow and leave it, but Duke Gravon's words haunt me, the topic of an attack. I keep on my cloak, the dagger tucked away inside as I feel reassurance having it. Do I expect someone here to attack me? No, I do not, but I fret that something else may. Perhaps an animal or some savage. I am surrounded by men heavily armed though, so why do I insist on having something to protect myself? It gives me a feeling I safety to know that I have a way to defend myself if things go wrong and if no one else can. The trail through the mountains is narrow, the fear of rocks dropping down on us making me only more uneasy. But I know we will soon be out of the danger of the mountains and seeing the Temple where so many of my questions can be answered.

"Lady Candice," King Kyril calls out, my eyes shifting from the high rocks above to the King. He walks in front of me, one of his trackers beside him as they have been talking for the past ten minutes about the Temple's architecture. "How well can you read Old Age Idunian?"

If I have been able to read Idunian already and can speak it very well, I should be able to. It all sounds and reads like English to me. "I trust that I can read it well," I reply, looking to the tracker beside the King who raises an eyebrow. He doubts me, meaning that this language must be very ancient. There is doubt and I am not sure if that is something I should accept as a challenge or know my limits of overestimating myself.

"Some like to think the Temple has a mind of its own," a voice comments from behind me, the familiar voice of Duke Gravon. "Stories have it that the Temple favors certain species more than others and if you're on its good side, then what you seek in those walls, you will find." The Temple never struck me as some magical place with a mind of its own, it only made an impact on me as a place where I landed in this realm.

"Why do they say that?" I ask, looking back to the Duke to see him opening an old journal.

"Elves are hated by the Temple. If an elf ventures in, then the elf will come out as if it's soul has been taken from its body. Vampires would often go missing in those walls, and when werewolves were sent in to find them, they could never even find a trace of them. Dragons love Temples built by the gods, but no dragon would dare fly close to this one."

"The Temple was built by a goddess five ages ago, a goddess who believed in different worlds beyond our own they could be reached if we wanted to," the tracker beside the King adds. "But it is a Temple forgotten by many, only remembered by old scholars and those who love a good puzzle."

"So, you think Heka has left clues in there?" I ask, looking beyond the path to see a small exit where trees stretch on for miles. "A trace of himself?"

The tracker nods. "The last activity in the Temple like this was reported when that thing first arrived in Iduna." The Temple's activity is of someone entering this realm. I was the person to cause the last activity, but no one needs to know this. "How do we know there could be a trace of him?"

The King stops, causing a whole chain reaction of his men stopping as well, everyone silent as they look to their King for his words. Turning around, his eyes lock with mine, his eyes swirling with dark shades of blue and green.

"That is what you are here for, correct, Lady Candice?" He asks, putting me on the spot as he seems cold to me suddenly.

I hold my head high. "Correct."

Chapter 12

Looking out at the Temple before me, it strikes me as unfamiliar. Yes, it is the same one I found myself waking up in as I was in a new world, but it seems so different now. Covered in snow, the Temple stands three stories tall, columns surrounding the large opening where stairs lead up to the entrance. It seems dark now, as if some sort of dark power has consumed it. Glancing to the King who looks to Duke Gravon, he seems on edge, nervous almost as he gives instructs and tells some of his men to guard the others that enter the Temple.

For me, I know I will be entering that Temple once more, but rather than nervous like many of these men, I feel relieved. I should be scared through, worried that the King may be on to me or that the Temple may suddenly not hold the answers that I seek in the form of my father's journal. As I take in a deep breath and dismount my horse as I see the King and some of his trackers do so, it is then that I begin to feel a bit nervous, every step I take my legs feeling unreliable. "Lady Candice, do not be afraid to lead the way," King Kyril informs, meeting my gaze as he motions for me to head for the Temple. It is not, not just to how he words it, but because of the look he gives me, the glance he spares me. He is supposed to lead his men in, not me, I am not their leader on this quest nor their King, but I simple female from a pack that cannot shift.

"Right away, my King," I reply, trying not to sound worried or on edge as I take my first steps forward, my cloak heavy as it rests on my shoulders, dragging behind as I pull it close, not for warmth, but for comfort as my nerves begin to act up. Letting out a deep breath, I take my steps forward, heading for the Temple as the King and his men follow in pursuit, looking to the Temple not with awe, but in fear. I heard just earlier of the rumors and events that this Temple is surrounded by, how many find it a fearful place depending on your species or perhaps even beliefs. As we approach the Temple, my palms become sweaty as I take my first steps upon the stairs, looking up to the entrance before me as the King walks close behind me, as if breathing down my neck. My legs carry me up the set of stairs heading into the Temple, King Kyril taking from the leather sash around his torso a small stone, throwing it into the air as he hums a tune.

The stone levitates in the air, lighting up the whole entrance of the Temple, displaying the exact location where I woke up what feels like hours ago. A simple Temple, but unlike last time when this place struck me as some minimal stone structure, this time it holds so much more than I had perceived. The same marble slab where I woke up is in the center of the room, the white marble polished as the sides hold a certain carving on it. But unlike last time, this time there are pink roses laid across the top, some of the petals having fallen to the floor, but the stems of the roses are all gathered in a lace ribbon, tied into a bow. This is not some random set of roses, but they were placed here for a reason, and as my skin growls pale and my eyes widen, I realize something none of these men must ever realize.

"What kind of flowers are those?" Duke Gravon asks, walking ahead of me and to the roses as he touches one of the flowers, examining it. "I have never seen these before."

"Roses," a random voice answers, causing every head to turn back to see a young man standing in the entrance. Carrying the flag of Kyril's kingdom, he bows his head to all of us, eyes briefly meeting mine as he offers us his insight. "These are roses, they grow in the Southern Mountains where I grew up."

"The Southern Mountains?" Duke Gravon asks, as if in disbelief. "Where the sun never shines and the dragons roam? What an off location, not to mention a five days journey on horse. A long journey for this person to lay these flowers here."

The young man hands the flag to a tracker, taking off the hood covering his face with a shadow, his bright blue eyes revealed as he looks to the flowers. "These flowers are new to my village, not like they started growing yesterday, but Heka brought them with him. These are the flowers he planted everywhere over the mountain range."

My father has been here. It is no surprise to me, that this is him, because these are the exact flowers he would give my mother for any event, whether it be her birthday, a holiday, or their anniversary. Besides, the ribbon as well, the way it is tied, it is a knot my mother showed me that my father discovered for his magic tricks, how you overlay the strands and pull them at different angles. My father either visits here and places these flowers down sometime...or he knows that I am here. He would know I am here because of the lightning strikes that called the King and his men here. My father would not expect anyone else to show up here besides someone in his family due to the fact he probably made the first portal or something, the same spawning point meaning to him that whoever entered Iduna came through the same mirror he did. That mirror is kept in the old house he once purchased for his family, only his wife and child having access to it.

"So Heka is closer than we thought," Kyril comments, looking around the entrance, and as he turns to the wall before the marble slab, his eyes catch his reflection in the mirror hanging from the wall. A mirror, one you would expect in Snow White, the shape it takes and the silver frame around it carved with precision. The King looks at his reflection, walking over to it as I find my throat running dry. That is the mirror that I came from and the mirror that I could possibly return home in. My eyes focus on the floor, looking around the floor for the journal, only, this is not the best timing. If my father got here before us, then he would have seen the journal, taking it with him. The journal is lost more than anything, in the hands of my father once more as I was a few days too late. Now what do I do? I expected to find that journal and it aid me in making these men trust me as well as for me to have an idea of where to search for my father. I check the floor for perhaps a journal that he left behind, as well as any sign to see where he has gone. "Lady Candice." My head perks up, looking to the King as he calls for me. He seems puzzled as he looks at his reflection in the mirror, head tilted as he lifts his hand up, meeting the solid mirror as his fingers press against the glass. A piece of me fears that his fingers will sink into the mirror and he will portal back to my house, but his fingers are not swallowed by the mirror. "Why would a Temple so sacred have a mirror? Why have an object that belongs in a bathroom hang in the main room of a Temple?"

I have no idea other than the mirror being the portal that brought me here. "My Lord?" I ask, walking around to where he stands, only to catch a glimpse at the engravings upon the sides of the marble slab, the once gibberish symbols translating right into a language I grew up reading. I stop walking, facing my entire attention upon the sides of the marble slab as the King and his men take notice.

"And so, the Lady can read ancient words lost in time," Duke Gravon comments, walking up to where I stand, examining the words on the slab as he cannot read what I am. They say these words are of some ancient language, but this is not ancient at all, but new. No, not days new, at least not all of it. This is a journal, some record book, English, and a signature at the end of each paragraph reading of the name of the man that my mother loved, and I called my father. They are dated too, all the way back to his first days here as he was trying to discover this realm and think of what all he would need. In the first entry he lists his fears of the creatures outside the Temple, how it was amazing to him the mountains surrounding the Temple, and how he was impressed his magic landed him in the exact spot he wanted to go.

I carry on, falling to my knees as I read the lower paragraphs too, eyes scanning quickly over everything as I cannot believe what I have just discovered here. My eyes stop, focusing on one journal entry dating back to only three days ago. How do I know it was just a few days ago? My father enters dates using the exact year and months that my home realm uses. This entry from a few days ago explains how he traveled here after rumors of a spell over the Temple, meaning that someone had traveled here. He talks of his journal from the Eastern Islands where the mermaids have claimed their domain and elves allow him to live beside them in peace. He talks of his excitement for someone from his home to have ventured here, but there is one thing that throws me off. My dearest Katerina, be safe in a world of wolves who can sniff out a traitor from a mile away. He writes to my mother, believing that it is not his own daughter that has come to find him, but the wife he left to suffer.

But it is not the part of the journals being written to my mother that throw me off, no, but the part about wolves being able to find a traitor from a long distance. My skin pales as I become nervous, rising to my feet as I look up to see the King and his men watching me. As I meet the King's stare, this time things feel off, as if I am seeing that he is not as blind as he looks.

"Discover anything, Lady Candice?" King Kyril asks, motioning towards the entries as I think of what to say.

I take in a shaky breath. "It seems that every time Heka visits this Temple he leaves a journal on the walls of this marble slab," I explain, telling the truth. "This first one discusses his first visit to Iduna. This one (his newest one) tells of his long journey from a village in the North, by a lake." I have no idea what the geography of the North is here. The King looks to Duke Gravon, as if awaiting some motion from the noble that watches me right now. "As to why he has left flowers here, I cannot tell why."

"How much time does Heka have ahead of us?" Duke Gravon asks, looking around to the trackers also in the room, a few of them holding up magnifiers to the marble walls, looking for any other writings. "How many days? Hours?" One man approaches the marble slab, picking up one of the roses, inspecting the flower as he looks to the stems, feeling them as my body remains tense. I am treading on thin ice and am close to falling in if not careful where I place my next footsteps. King Kyril walks around the marble slab, standing beside me as he too looks at the writings. Fingers running along the carved words, he reaches into some pocket, pulling out what looks like a paintbrush, a gold handle, flaming red thin feathers on the end as it reminds me of some holiday-themed makeup brush. "Would a phoenix feather help? We have tired this before on older words, my King, but it rarely works on these."

A phoenix feather helps translate. How would it do that? "Duke Gravon, phoenix feathers translate an Idunian language dating back to creation when their first forms roamed the land. If this is an Idunian language, it will translate." But this language is not Idunian. This language is nothing from this realm, but my own. Due to only reading Idunian for the past so many days as well as speaking it, looking to a language I grew up studying took a little to adjust to, but as I look at it now, I can see it is Arabic. The phoenix wand that the King holds will be unable to translate this because it is not Idunian, meaning that these men will want an explanation for how I was able to read it.

"My King," I state, looking to the King who holds the tip of the feathers over the first few letters. "The feathers will not work because the language is not from Iduna, but from Heka's world," I inform, knowing I need to step up and make sure I do not fall through the ice and face my death today. "When Heka came to my pack, this is a language that he taught me as well as other children how to read."

Kyril puts his want away, shaking his head as he grabs a handful of the roses, his hand opening as a fire ignites and the roses turn to ashes in a blue flame. As the eyes of the King meet mine, I am met with a color of eyes that mirror those of the phoenix feathers, bright red with streaking of orange and gold that flicker just as flames would. The King does not look pleased, setting his hand upon the marble slab as flames engulf the top, swallowing whole the flowers in high and dangerous flames you would expect from a bonfire. This is not a man I want to upset more than I have already. Looking to the roses that have become nothing but part of the fire now, the slab I woke up on is not something I wish to touch again.

"Enough is enough, my King," Duke Gravon shouts, throwing out his hands into the air as the flames vanish with a gust of cold air, only smoke emerging from the slab as the white marble is stained in a black layer from the past fire. "Throwing a small fit will not get us closer to this savage." Small fit? That was nothing close to some small fit you would throw. "What we need is a set plan to find this male. Going about only looking for sightings or signs and giving up when we seem to have approached a dead end will get us nowhere."

"And what would you suggest, Duke?" Kyril asks, his voice deep, as if some animistic growl. "Tear the surface of Iduna apart until we find this traitor?"

The Duke shakes his head, looking to me as my skin pales. "We trace back to Heka's first movements. Lady Candice was taught by Heka as well as several children from her pack when Heka first arrived. We should go back to Lady Candice's pack and see if those children like Lady Candice would be able to help us."

No. King Kyril will be the one to decapitate me before the sun could even set when he finds out what I am and who I am the daughter of. There are no others like me and there is no pack from which I am from. These men cannot know it. I have an idea of where my father is but venturing there without proper transportation or even a sense of direction or defense means I would be dead before I would get close to my father. I had hoped that I would split with the King and his men after this day, to get a horse and money for the voyage I would take back to some made up pack. I would be gone by the end of the day towards my father had things gone planned.

"Lady Candice, how would your pack feel about a visit from their King?" Kyril asks, meeting my gaze as I try not to look like a deer in the headlights. "We leave in the morning for Lady Candice's pack and to trace this savage down." I want to shake my head and say no, but that would me walking to the sword to cut off my head. Taking in a deep breath, I nod my head, only, as I look to the trackers realizing a long journey than expected is underway, I look to the mirror. Unlike the King or anyone before who had looked into this mirror, I do not see a reflection of myself to reflect on and question my ways, but I see a portal right back into my father's office. And there, standing before the mirror as she sits at my father's desk, my mother has a bottle of vodka at her side, a pen in her hand, and her hair a mess as she works frantically.

So close. So close yet so far away. My eyes become drawn into the portal as I see in one of her hands a compass, one with Arabic on the sides, my mother screaming at the top of her lungs as she throws the alcohol at the other side of the room, crashing as I want to go back to her, reach out, comfort her and tell her that father thinks she is here now and that he wants her to come and find him.

"Lady Candice?" I snap back to the reality I am now faced with, meeting the stare of the King of his men begin to exit the Temple, the Duke about to leave as King Kyril and I are left alone in the Temple. "Are you coming?" I nod, looking back to the mirror as the King begins to walk for the entrance. My mother is on her feet now, pacing around the room as tears stream down her face. Is it selfish of me to stay here while she can barely keep herself sane back home? If I left Iduna and went home, to mend the relationship I have with my mother, to tell her of the world of Iduna and that father is alive, we could come back here one day together to find my father, to find the missing puzzle of our family. It could work, but that would mean I would have to give up right now and go back home to the mess my mother has become. But I must face the harsh truth that if I follow the King out of the Temple he will expect me to show him and his men my pack which I have no idea where to even start with that. I could die in the next few hours or days, but if I return home with my mother right now, I could live another day, be with my mother, and one day return with her back here to find the man that left our lives and we still have hope will return.

Looking over my shoulder to see the King gone, I take in a shaky breath, throwing the fur cloak off my shoulders as I stand in the Temple with a dress and dagger in my hands as I know my mother will think my attire very odd. Undoing the braids my hair is pinned up in, I take a step towards the mirror, closing my eyes as I accept the plan I shall now follow through with. My father has lived this long without his family, he can live another day or month without us. Just as I reach out my hand and feel the liquid mirror, a force runs into my body, knocking me down as the dagger in my hand skids across the floor.

My eyes shoot open to see the King holding me down, one of his hands holding mine over my head as I try and push him off, unable to as he looks closer at me, face close to mine as his lips brush my cheek. "Another human to enter Iduna, how peculiar," he comments, a sly tone to his voice as my heart pounds in my chest.

"Another human I would have no trouble killing right now, but the gods must have some sick sense of humor, do you not agree."

"Get off me you monster," I snap, raising my head up as I bite into the King's neck, trying to do him and form of harm. The King only growls, straddling me as he pulls his face away, his free hand reaching up to his neck. Pulling his hand back and looking to the blood present, his darkening eyes move to mine.

"The moment you walked into my palace I knew what you were, but your angelic face and the fact that we are somehow mates got the best of me and I allowed instinct to take charge. I cannot simply disregard the fact that you are human, but that fact that you are my mate, Candice, is the sole reason for why you will never go near this mirror again."

I get one hand free, my fist colliding with his jaw as I am loose, springing for the dagger Duke Gravon gifted me just hours ago. The hilt in my hand as my fingers wrap around the cold metal and I take a large swing, pointing the dagger right at the King as he is crocheted over still where I left him, hand feeling around the location of his jaw that I hit. "Let me go and I will never give you harm again," I inform, rising to my feet as the King does the same. "I do not intent to harm you, but if that is what I must do to return to my home, then you bet I will harm you."

"I would not dare allow a day to go by without you by my side, Candice, and I would destroy the heavens to do so," Kyril growls, standing before the mirror and me as my heartbeat runs faster than ever before. "Why are you trying to find Heka? Was your journey here unplanned? Was finding me unplanned? Or are you not just some random human that happens to be from his world?" I hold my head high, looking to the mirror to see my mother once again, inspecting a piece of my father's collections upon a bookshelf.

My jaw is clenched as I try and think of how to respond. "He is nothing to me but a fellow human," I snap, taking a step forward as I recall my footing from my years of fencing back home. My dagger raised, and my knees bent, I look my opponent in the eye, taking in a steady breath as I am ready to fight this werewolf and god knows what else. "Now pick up your sword and let us settle this." I know he will not fight me, I am not foolish. He will not harm me because he believes us to be soulmates. I on the other hand...that word means nothing to me. The King draws his sword like I expected, acting all high and mighty as he drops his cloak to the floor and raises his sword. His sword may be longer than mine, but I know I was a goddamn good fencer back when I did it. Just as I take my first step towards him in attack mode, the King turns around, facing the mirror as he raises his sword.

"No," I scream, dropping my dagger as I jump onto his back, grabbing his sword as I fling it from his hands, my arms around his neck as I hook my legs around his waist, using my momentum to bring us both crashing into the floor. My shoulder takes the fall, pain erupting in my shoulder and back as the King turns around, pinning me down once more, his fingers running through my hair as he cocks his head to the side and offers me a sly smile. "Please do not break it," I plead, knowing he will not give me mercy, but I use my phrase as a chance to stretch out the time, raising my head as I land it hard against his own. As he releases me, I run for the mirror, my fingertips just brushing the fabrication of the portal back to my home, only for my body to be thrown across the hall.

My body collides with the opposite wall from the mirror, my screams filling the air as I fall to my knees, watching as Kyril's fist collide with the mirror, the glass shattering into millions of tiny pieces, unable to ever be put back together. Tears stream down my face as Kyril looks over his shoulder to me, his eyes black as he stands in the shadows of the room, blood on his fists, and a darkness drawn to him.

I can never go home...and he could not be happier.

Chapter 13

My body is weak, worn out, my hands receiving the bitter numbing pain of the cold as my wrists are bound together by rope, walking behind the King as his men follow us in pursuit. We walk through the camp, already my tent taken down as news has reached the camp of my traitor status. Traitor but not human status. King Kyril informed his men that I was speaking nonsense, telling them that I joined the race to find Heka as an attempt to steal goods from the King and make a run for it into the mountains.

The men bought the lie, believing their King as he could not tell them I was human. I was only a fraud in who I claimed I was, not what I said I could do. My legs weak from the hike and the events of my body being thrown across a hall just an our ago, as the King stops walking, he turns back to me, placing a hand on my shoulder as he guides me into his tent, leaving the rest of his men outside. As my throat runs dry, I try and hold my head high, knowing that I am about to stand up for myself and come up with a reason for why I am trying to find Heka aside from him being my father. With the tent isolating us from the rest of the camp, King Kyril lets go of my shoulders, taking a seat on his bed as he looks at me, running his hands through his hair. "How does a human like yourself end up in Iduna?"

I expected harsh words to be said, for my body to be flung about the room, for my eyes to water and for Kyril to shout at me. Rather than any of that, he asks me a simple question, his voice not raised at all, but calm. Like the calm before the storm. "I found a mirror the day I was sucked into this realm," I inform, taking in a deep breath as I need this to be believable. I am good with lies, all the way through elementary school I would tell people that my mother was always around for my ceremonies and holiday festivities, that she never missed one. I would create elaborate stories as for why no one saw her and they all believed me. "I found myself in that Temple and that same day of me waking up in there, I met a woman from the mountains. She told me of another human who had passed by before, of a man named Heka." He is buying it, the way he shakes his head. "I asked her how to find Heka and she said she knew a man that could get me into your palace records library to perhaps find the last sighting of him."

"And so you wanted to be added to the race to find Heka in hopes of finding him," the King pieces together, looking up to me with glowing golden eyes. "To find a way to return home?"

I nod, watching as the King rises to his feet, grabbing a glass as he fills it with a rick blue substance, taking a swing at the drink. "And that mirror was my last chance to return home because who knows where Heka is or if he even knows a way for me to see my family again," I add, my voice raised as I want to pounce onto the King, wrap my hands around his neck and squeeze tight. "In the mirror, right before you destroyed it, I saw my mother, drinking away her sorrows as she was left with no one but herself for company." Pathos. Just tons of pathos right now and he should find sympathy for me and give me some freedom to move around. "I do not give a damn about you wanting the kill Heka, but I want to find him just as badly as you do. You know that you need me to find him, that I am the only one who can read his language because I was born in his world. Your magic has no use in finding him, the only way you can find him is by another human. I happen to be that human."

King Kyril scoffs, shaking his head as he looks down to me, his shadow looming over me as he takes a swing at his drink again. "You see, dear little Candice, the last time we spoke like this you were persuading me to add you to the race while lying to me about your background. A silver tongue you have perhaps once more?"

I take in a deep breath, one to gain the confidence to say my words. "It doesn't matter anymore, any of my background or my motives, but you know that without me, you have no chance of finding Heka."

"So you can return home?" the King asks, his tone mocking me. "You are my mate, Candice, so that means I will be damned if you talk to Heka because I will never allow you to return home."

Red, all I see is red. Lunging for the King, I know my hands are tied, but I do not care, wrapping my legs around his waist as I jump, I just my tied-up hands to land a hard punch right to the King's nose, the sound of the cartilage breaking. The King growls, the power of the sound shaking the tent as I find myself thrown off of the King, landing onto the soft mattress of the bed. As he comes for me, I act fast, rolling off of the cot and onto the floor as I quickly get to my feet, eyes briefly meeting the King's as his eyes darken. The sword he keeps on his nightstand, I press the rope against the blade, cutting fast as the King lunges for me once more, but this time, I have a sword. "You are never going home, Candice, but staying here with me," the King growls, taking a careful step back as I raise the sword, my knees bent.

"I would be careful, King, because I took lessons with swords and I was very good," I inform, recalling my fencing days as I am glad that my private school at least offered that as my chance to get out of doing gym. My father had a gift for swords, and although he may have swallowed them most of the time for tricks, mother would tell me of a story involving him that could have come right out of an Indiana Jones movie. "We both know we need one another to find Heka, although what we want with him is very different. You want him dead and I want him alive. You want me to stay here and I want to go home. Let me ask you, do you honestly believe that soul mates can last, and if so, are we even soul mates? You said the gods must be playing a joke on you, and if they are, you do not want me, a human, but your side for the rest of your life."

Grabbing his own sword, the King raises his, eyes glazed over as I hold my head high. "You will never leave Iduna," he snaps, walking forward as I stand my ground, sword raised for a battle as the King puts on a mask. He would never dare harm me with a duel, no, this is all just a game for him, for him to make me think he could harm me and for me to drop my weapon. I am not like the King, for the word soul mate has no definition to me but some cheesy word people use as an excuse in relationships. "That mirror was your only chance to get out and now it is gone. Heka would never even dare help you, seeing that he is a traitor and liar after all. Heka is selfish." All I see is red as I take my first swing, our swords colliding with one another. I know what role he takes here, as he is on defense and I am on offense. He will not a harmful swing at me, no, only a warning one to try and scare me off.

I spin around, raising my sword up and bringing it down with a fast momentum, Kyril quickly leaping back, sticking out his sword to catch mine from landing straight into his bed. "I will return home, you bastard," I yell, lunging forward, and as I do so, I drop to my knees, my left leg sticking out as I swing it around, taking the King out from under his feet. As he lands on the ground, I move fast, knocking his sword out of his hand and keeping the tip of my blade right against his jugular vein. "Stay away from me," I hiss, bring my sword up, only to bring the hilt of my sword down to hit his head, only, a force holds me back.

I'm pushed away, the King holding up his hand as a glowing blue sphere is in his hand, sparks going off around the orb as the King's eyes glow the exact same color. "Know who you are messing with, Candice, for you seem to forget this world is of magic," he states, walking forward as I stand unable to move next to a tapestry upon the tent wall. It is a tapestry of the very assassination my father was part of, him holding a bow and launching an arrow that lands in the chest of the male who wears the crown. How ironic that I almost followed in my father's footsteps and could have just decapitated this King. "Heka was wise unlike you, a human that understood the tricks we Idunians have hidden up our sleeves. You see, species can mate with species and from that, you can either receive mutated beings with demonic features and making the quality of life for them miserable, or you can have something like me." He refers to himself as something, as if some unknown creature that children are afraid of. "Something that the heavens cower from and the pits of hell look up to. I am not just some species that can become a wolf when I please, but something unreal. Heka knew this, he knew who my real mother was and did not dare mess with me."

"So, the little Kyril's father had an affair and you were born from that," I point out, feeling the hairs raise on the back of my neck as Kyril gets closer. "What was your mother, an elf?" I know from Soka that elves are not to be associated with, that they have an evil demeanor, and no one wants to work alongside them.

My body is thrown to the floor, a force keeping me down as I find it hard to raise my neck and look to anticipate what happens next. "I doubt you have ever seen a dragon in Iduna yet."

"Let me guess, you mom was the mother of dragons and had platinum blond hair?"

My head becomes dizzy, my fingers beginning to numb, and as Kyril crouches down, he places two fingers under my chin, lifting my head up to meet his glowing blue orbs. "I guess you could say that, after all, she did craft them from her very hands and breath fire into their souls."

His mother is the goddess that created dragons. He is a demigod, but not like in Percy Jackson where they are half god and half human, no, Kyril is half god and half werewolf, a recipe for fear. The fire makes sense, the one he set in the Temple that consumed all of the flowers on the slab. Could the sparks that I feel when he touches me be because of that as well? He says that the sparks are a sign of us being mates, but that could be just because he is able to use fire as some weapon of choice. "My mother had always wanted a son. She had a daughter that perished in battle eons ago, one that was half enchantress. My sister was powerful, stories still told about her adventures, but she was weak in the end, an arrow in her thigh, laced with poison. She allowed herself to die without even trying to rid her blood of the substance. Mother waited eons to find another male suitable for giving her a powerful offspring, so when my father came along, she knew I would be a child of wonder and a storm to be feared."

My eyes are wide, looking to the blue orb still in his hand, still glowing and making sparks as I fear it getting too close for comfort. Looking back to Kyril, a smile begins to spread across his face, one that makes my skin pale and my mouth have a sour taste. "I think it is time we go and see my mother, do you not agree, Candice?"

"By all means, lead the way," I state, my vice stern and sarcastic as I know that I need to get out of here as soon as possible.

"Then the two of us leave at sundown."

The King moves, grabbing my arms, lifting me to my feet as I feel the sparks the moment his skin contacts mine. Fear is laced through every inch of my body, looking back to the tapestry of my father slaying Kyril's father, my father's face masked by a pair of black horns and red eyes, a serpent's tongue stretching out of his mouth as his hands that grasp the bow have talons. I am led from the tent, the cold wind meeting my skin as Duke Gravon stands before the tent, eyes meeting mine. But he does not look at me like the rest of the men here, how they have stares that makes me fear they will try and harm me. No, not Duke Gravon, for his eyes hold a soft sparkle of some sorts, his face not stern and lips pressed together in a firm line, but he looks like he is wearing a mask. Perhaps I could find an ally as well as a friend in Duke Gravon if I am given the opportunity to. Kyril trusts the Duke very much, respecting him even, which makes me think that perhaps Duke Gravon could be the Brutus to Kyril's Caesar. Mostly likely not, but I know Duke Gravon does not think me to be the traitor Kyril told his men I was. The Duke sees something in me and I do not yet know if that is wise to place trust in.

"Duke Gravon, have my men ready three horses with food and water for a two-day journey," Kyril instructs, grabbing hold of one of my elbows tightly, pulling me further from the tent.

"May I ask who the third companion may be?" The Duke asks, looking to me, offering me a slight nod as Kyril is distracted by looking towards a few of his men pitching a small tent.

As the King looks back, he pulls me closer to his frame, looking to the sun as I see that we will be heading out soon. "You will, Gravon." Kyril pulls me with him away from the Duke and towards the small entrance where we were just earlier when heading to the Temple. With my feet finding it hard to keep up with the King's long strides, the chilling air causes my nose to numb and fingers feel pain from the icy weather, my body shivering as he only pulls me further through the narrow valley of rocks. "Tell me, my dear Lady Candice, why should I trust a word you have spoken about what the marble slab read, of Heka having made journals." We come to a sudden halt, the King pushing me up against a rocky wall, my back uncomfortable as my eyes shoot to the rocks above, afraid that they will fall and crush my small frame. What a way to go. "Please enlighten me."

"Because it is true, those were journal entries for every time he ventured back to the Temple. Heka comes from my world, from me country where English is the language spoken in and written in, meaning that I was able to translate the entries with no struggle. Your phoenix feather has no power there. I am your only chance at reading those journals, so you better believe me," I reply, my voice stern and monotone, eyes locked with a set of dark blue and purple orbs, hoping that he believes me because it is the truth. "That is what the marble slab held and what it only held. He wrote to his wife in one, telling her of his love for her." Kyril's hands once pressed upon my shoulders pull back, letting out a deep sigh as I hold my head high. "You believe me or you do not, but no matter what, you cannot deny I am the only one who can read those words."

The King looks to me from the corner of his eyes as he looks back to where the camp is located in the distance. "I take it that in your world men and women are held at the same respects."

"The idea is there, but many men like yourself are too stubborn to accept the equality of the sexes," I inform, "I do not give a damn about some title you were given due to your bloodline, Kyril, but I do give a damn about seeing my mother and father again."

"I have already informed you that will never happen," Kyril snaps, hands on my waist as he holds me tight against the wall of rocks.

I shove at the King, hands pushing against his chest as he does not budge. "We will just have to see about that," I reply, my elbow landing hard into the King's chest, the King stumbling back, only, he grabs my arm in the process, taking me with him to the ground as I use this sudden motion to swing my body on top of his, taking hold of his shirt in my fists as I lean forward, lips close to his as I cock my head to the right. "Be careful, my King, for many are foolish to underestimate the underdog and before they realize their mistake, the underdog has beat them at their own game."

I rise to my feet, walking away from the King and towards the camp as I know it is no use running towards the Temple. There is no use running anywhere because this man can use magic. Sure, I could knock him out cold, at least I think so, but his men could come after me or he could dodge the blow by using some magical power. I just have to be one step ahead of this man the entire journey to find my father. I will have to learn to Gravon the most I can about magic, about things I could one day use to get away from Kyril, perhaps potions or words that could be of use. As I approach the camp once more and Duke Gravon is there to greet me, I offer him a soft smile, one of friendliness. "The King will be right back, he is just gathering his pride," I inform, hearing a few laughs come from the soldiers by the King's tent, finding what I say to be entertaining. It shows that the respect I thought that they held for the King is a little unsteady, finding funny how they see their King values his pride. Perhaps this is a sign that the underdog has just found a way to stay one step ahead of her competition.

"Perhaps it is for the best," Duke Gravon adds, offering me the same cloak I had worn before, the fur from a fox. Perhaps irony, how a fox is seen as a sly creature, a deceiver, one to always have a trick up its sleeve. Perhaps I am the fox as well, to take out the high and mighty King from the inside rather than an attack from the outer walls.

Smiling, I thank the Duke, putting the cloak on, and as the sides of the material hit my side, a solid object hits my hipbone. Looking to the inner pocket, the Duke has placed the dagger he gifted me with before back in the cloak for safe keeping. "Use it well, Lady Candice," he whispers, walking off just as the King appears from the mist of the mountain passage. As his eyes connect with mine, I no longer look at a male that I am scared of, but one that I cannot wait to dance a dangerous game with.

Chapter 14

As the horses have become loaded up and I find my fingers numb from the chilling air, I look ahead to the path that only leads upwards, straying farther away from both the camp and the Temple: the only two places I can memorize my way around in this new world. With my body covered in the same cloak that reminds me of a fox, my horse covers the rough terrain of the side of the mountains with ease, the reigns of the horse tied to a rope that is attached to Duke Gravon's own horse. With what I know to be a three-day journey total, the horses are packed lightly, the food and water having passed the King's approval for the trip as he wanted to leave as soon as the sun was beginning to fall into the ground. As my eyes flicker to the male who I seem to only trust on this trek, he hands me a warm mug, steam rising from the surface as the mug warms up my hands the moment they wrap around the cylinder.

Thanking the Duke, I take a long drink from the mug, welcoming the warmth of the liquid that reminds me of an herbal tea my mother used to make. It has only been at most an hour since I last saw sight of the camp that reminds me at least as a source of warmth and haven. But now I am out in the great unknown once more, surrounded by only two males who are not human, and on a journey to speak with some goddess. To think a month ago I was in my home, wrapped in the welcoming covers of my bed, the glowing light of my phone illuminating my room as I would chat with good friends about what the future would hold for us or reflect on memories that brought a smile to my face. Funny how things can be taken for granted and next thing you know, you are tossed into unfamiliar territory.

"Duke Gravon, how far away is the Temple to this goddess?" I ask, recalling how the Duke informed me a day ago about the Temples, about how they were built for the gods and goddess where worshipers could speak with their deity.

"Dregh?" The Duke asks, his horse slowing down so ours are walking beside one another, allowing for a more personal conversation. Looking from the Duke quickly, I see the King ahead of us by a few meters, concentrated on the path ahead as he seems to be consumed in the world of his mind. "We are not headed to her Temple, no, for that would mean we would be sailing across the oceans for a week before reaching the volcano where here Temple is built." So, they have volcanos here. It makes sense for a goddess of fire or dragons to have her Temple built upon the surface of a volcano although I would not wish to step foot on a volcano.

"Children of the gods and goddess, they can seek communication with their parents by casting a simple spell at a high peak." It makes sense for why we are headed up the mountains then, to reach a high peak where the King can perform a spell to summon his mother. I remember Soka telling me of dragons, of how they keep to themselves for the most part unless disturbed, telling me it would be very rare for me to every meet one, yet here I am, to meet the goddess of dragons within a few days. Growing up, I found dragons to be mere creatures of someone's imagination from long ago, creatures that I found to be impressive when movies portrayed them with heavy computer-generated images. As a child, dragons were what I wanted to reach about when my mother's maid would tuck me in for bed because my mother had locked herself away in my father's office or was out on another one of her trips.

"Why must we speak to his mother? Why does he not do this on his own?" I ask, taking a sip once more at the drink in my hands. The Duke looks to his King, simply shrugging his shoulders as he takes the reigns of his horse, causing it to slow down as mine does as well. The King still looks lost in his own world, not once glancing back to us at all. He made sure my horse was tied up to the Duke's in case of escape, but he does underestimate me there. I would not be dumb enough to run off when these men could easily catch up to me because I am just human and have no sense of direction in this world. If I wanted to escape, I would be smart about it, not putting my survival on the line whatsoever.

"My guess, Lady Candice, is he has plans for you with his mother." I raise an eyebrow, looking from the Duke and to the path ahead of us, the path only becoming steeper the farther we travel in the winter chill. "For a child to reach out to their deity parent, it is often frowned upon in the ancient books dating back to the creation of Iduna."

"You make it seem like Iduna is eons old," I comment, recalling an old conversation that Soka once held with me when I had asked about humans. She told me that in the ancient days that humans would hunt down the supernatural species for sport or for what they believed to be defense, driving the supernatural to low numbers. If humans and the people of Iduna once lived in the same universe or realm, could it be that the gods or goddesses could be the last supernatural to live among humans before creating this realm of harmony? From what I have seen in my time in Iduna, they are stuck in some medieval age, perhaps an indication that Iduna was built at this time and the world has never been able to progress with things like electricity or thought like back in the world I am from.

The Duke nods, agreeing with my comment. "It is very old, years and years as far as time can stretch back and all there was in the universe was a darkness. Did the elders of your community not teach you these things?" Duke Gravon asks, looking puzzled as he reflects on all the questions I have asked. "Did your elders teach differently." Only Kyril knows me to be human here, not Duke Gravon, or anyone else back at that camp. Asking too many questions could cause someone to question me, seeing how the Duke already is confused by my questions, wondering why my pack or community never taught me such things.

"My mother never focused much on teaching my siblings and me the history of Iduna," I inform, recalling how Kyril told the entire camp that I was a traitor and not a word I could say could be accounted for as trustworthy. Duke Gravon may be doubting my story right now, but he is not dumb, even someone who is willing to overlook the words of his King if he sees something to not be true. The Duke may question me with my background where I have said I grew up, but he is not someone to associate every word I speak with the words of a liar. "My mother focused on the future, on her daughters to grow up not in the shadow of men, but as individuals as influential and powerful as the opposite sex."

"Thus, you speak not just to the average male as if there is no status difference, but even to your King." I nod, finishing off the mug of tea and handing it back to the Duke. "It truly is a different way of thinking, and I take it then that your mother taught you how to properly use a sword?"

"Yes, she did." Not entirely false, for my mother signed me up for fencing lessons, allowing me to learn the skill. Although she did not teach me like the Duke thinks, she paid for those classes. One of the few awards ceremonies that she ever attended was for one of my tournaments where I placed second, one of the few times I was proud of my mother for trying to be a family. Kyril took that chance away from me to go back to her, to be there for her.

I had thought she would be fine without me seeing that she has always been without me, that she would be out on another trip trying to find her husband and perhaps even daughter. But seeing her in my father's office, drinking away the pain, and trying to figure things out, it made me want to banish the thought of finding my father and just return home to her. Sure, my family has never been tightly knit since my father left, but that does not mean my loyalty does not belong to my family. Every family has problems, has that one person or perhaps even everyone that drives you insane e as the family crumbles. Yes, there are some things that are unforgivable and make you lose all loyalty for someone, but that is hardly the case. We all fight, all hate someone at some time, but being flesh and blood, being raised by these people, living your life among these people, you find that your loyalty dwells with them.

My mother may have hardly been present in my life, but she is the woman that birthed me, who raised me, who taught me the things I never knew, who paid for my expansion of knowledge, and who sits all alone in the house once filled with her loved ones, wondering if my father or I are even alive at this point. My mother has been loyal her whole time to my father, eleven years after his disappearance still trying to find him.

"The King tries not to disturb his mother," Duke Gravon points out, drawing me away from my thoughts as my eyes lock to the back of the King, to the black locks upon his head, the contour of his back as you can tell that underneath all the layers of his clothes, he was built to take down kingdoms and rule with an iron fist. He is a man with a strong determination to kill my father, but my devotion to my father is much stronger than his sheer will to slay my father. But this could be a testimony of the King's own loyalty to his family, to the father of his that was murdered by my own. Even if soul mates were a thing and what the King said about the two of us were true, he would be right: fate has a sick sense of humor. "The gods and especially the goddesses to not care to be bothered, especially by their children."

"So why produce an offspring if they care not for a parent-child relationship?" No wonder why Kyril called the woman who married is father his mother rather than his actual birth mother. The woman that married his father acted as a mother to him, helped raise him, and died beside him was more of a mother to him than the goddess who wanted to have a strong offspring for some reason.

The Duke shrugs his shoulders, taking a quick look to the King, as if not wanting him to overhear his next words.

"It is because the gods and goddesses have this bet going, one of who can produce the strongest child. We are like gladiators," Kyril responds, halting his horse as he looks over his shoulder to us. "We are gladiators, ones who they train by giving us powers to learn how to us. They invest in us, how they find a suitable partner to produce a strong offspring as well as raise us. The gods like to see how well we demigods survive when tasks are placed before us."

"So, they have children as a competition to see whose child will become the strongest?" I ask, Kyril offering me a simple nod to confirm my question. "So that is why your sister, the one who died in battle-

"Dregh, my deity mother, mated with a strong warrior for my sister, only to become disappointed when she died in battle. Dregh saw her as weak and then turned her eyes to royals in the werewolf world. When my father came to power and was given the crown, she saw greatness in him and decided that their offspring would be valuable."

"So, you are just a piece of entertainment for the gods?" I ask, the Duke immediately choking on air at the bluntness of my question. "Entertainment that they invest in and then watch."

The King allows a smile to dance across his face, tugging upwards at the corner of his lips as a dimple on his left cheek appears. "Years ago, there were many demigods born, born to fight one another just like gladiators in an arena. Compared to what those demigods had to go through, I get the royal treatment, literally even." Kyril turns his horse around, facing us now as he has the horse approach us, eyes locked to mine as my throat runs dry. "The winners were gifted with a Kingdom to rule. My father, his great-great-grandfather was a demigod of the goddess Selene, a very powerful werewolf, and after winning the gods' game, he was given a Kingdom in which one day consumed Iduna. So here I am, the King of Iduna and the child of Dregh as well as having the blood of Selene in me." Selene, the goddess or werewolves or something if I can recall all the teen books I had read.

"What of the others like you, the other demigods?" I ask, watch as the King undoes the side of the rope attached to the Duke's horse and ties it around his horse's reigns, my horse now tied to his.

Silence, only the sound of the powerful winds from the mountains consuming us. "Heka happened to them," Duke Gravon responds rather than the King. "Heka found every child holding blood from a god or goddess and slayed them, but when he came to the palace, he believed King Kyril's father to be the demigod, slaying him rather than the son of Dregh." My skin pales, learning more of my father's time spent here in Iduna. While my mother and I have been living without him, he has been slaying demigods. "Many of those demigods were children, unable to use their powers yet, and if they could, Heka simply cast some sort of spell never seen in this realm before." My father slayed children, innocent little children all for what? What was his motive? There must be some motive. Perhaps something that may even validate his actions...but nothing could justify the butchery an innocent child.

"Why?"

My horse is tugged forward as the King starts back on the path, bringing an end to our conversation as we leave the Duke behind us to follow. With the King by my side, I feel his eyes preying upon me, taking in every feature of mine a I want an answer to my question, but something tells me I will have to do more than ask to get the answers I seek. Perhaps Duke Gravon could answer for me, but something tells me this is a question for Kyril, for him to have the true motivation answer already in that strange head of his.

As the darkness of the night takes over and the temperature drops lower than I have ever experienced before, and the stars are brighter than ever, Duke Gravon and the King begin pitching our camp for the night, just three small cots with fur blankets surrounding a fire. Nothing close to luxury at all. With the camp all set up, just as I go to take a cot for the night, the King draws a circle around our camp with his sword, sprinkling a golden ask in the grooves mad in the snow, whispering unfamiliar words. Once the King comes full circle with the golden ash, I stare in awe as a globe forms around our camp, the snow no longer falling into it, a thin, light blue seal around the camp as the warmth is contained. Magic to say the least.

Taking my cot for the night, comfort is all I feel as I lay on my back, staring up at the stars that flood the night sky. We have been traveling for many hours and just not sitting on a horse makes me feel happier than ever. Just as my eyelids become heavy and I drift off, I catch a sign, one that informs me that my prediction of the supernatural of Iduna and my own world once being one world may just be correct. The Little Dipper, a constellation that as a child I loved to look at, is in the night sky, bight as my eyes dance across every constellation in the sky. My eyes widen as I recall every constellation in the sky, my heart rate going crazy as my home may not be as far away as I believe it to be.

"Candice?" Turning my head to the left, I meet the soft gaze of the King, time freezing for a few seconds as he offers me a small smile. "Good night."

As he looks away and shuffles in his cot to get more comfortable, a smile forms on my face as well, biting my lower lip as I cannot contain my excitement. My excitement for the realization of how familiar the sky looks to me now. Perhaps there is another way out of here besides that mirror, perhaps it is just finding the end of Iduna where my world could be just beyond some globe like the globe that surrounds our camp. Perhaps I am closer to my mother than I ever thought, and it is just a matter of time before I am back to seeing her.

Taking in a deep breath, I shut my eyes for the night, no longer never to return to my home.

Chapter 15

I f anything, the fact that having to climb to the top of the highest mountain in the area has not made my day at all, rather crushing my spirits even more as the Duke tied our horses down to a tree a few miles back as the trail got too dangerous. It is not the fact that that the cliff beside where I walk is a plummet into an endless abyss, but that the weather has begun to change ever since our trio left our horses.

No, the weather has not just changed in temperature or the snow falling, but the clouds...the clouds swirl around the peak of the mountain we are headed to, the clouds seeming to glow golden, lightning strikes not running vertical, but horizontally in the sky. Duke Gravon said it is because a demigod is reaching out to his mother, to a goddess that crafted the most dangerous beasts of the realm and struck fear into the heavens and hell. As I look away from the frightening sky and to the landscape surrounding us, the other mountains hold no comparison to the one we are hiking upon, the trees below like ants, the frozen rivers looking like cracks in an artist's painting, and the white stone Temple looks like nothing more but a pebble.

"Tell me, Lady Candice, have you ever been up to such heights?" Duke Gravon asks, looking down to the abyss with me. If I was completely honest I would say that I have flown in the skies, a passport in my bag and a ticket allowing me to fly from the city I grew up in to halfway across the world. I remember that time my mother took me with her on one of her adventures, how we stopped in India, and while I wanted to indulge myself in the culture, mother was on an archaeological dig, leaving me with a hired nanny to make sure I stayed within the limits of my mother's orders. That was the first time I saw my mother in her natural habitat, dressed from head to toe in what you would expect an archaeologist to wear, her headphones drowning out the voices around her, and a certain atmosphere around her.

That trip was the first time I had ever heard her not just yell at others, but yell at me, telling me to stay out of her business when I asked her if I could go out and explore one of the local sights. I was just twelve when I smelled strong alcohol on her breath and expected her to hit me for some impatience. I swore I would never go on a trip with her ever again, nor did she ever ask me anyway. I only went with her because her sister urged her to spend time with me rather than me spend my summer break at some boarding school where I learned to appreciate the arts.

Have I forgiven my mother for all the times she shut me out and wanted to forget the world around her? I have, I have because I love my mother, because even if it may seem like she never loves or would even care for me, she does. She is the woman who brought me into this world and she is my family, my flesh and blood, and nothing could take that away from me. But she is delusional in a sense, to that my father and her husband may return home before she decides to shut out his memory forever.

"I am afraid not, Duke Gravon," I reply, peering over the cliff even more as I see the dirt moving from under my foot, heading for the cliff, falling off and into the dark abyss where time seems to not exist. "There are not many mountains from the territory of my pack." I still must play along with my being werewolf, at least not in front of the King as he knows exactly what I am. As for who I am, I pray that he never finds out.

"Dragons are not the gentlest creature to ride upon, their scales digging into your flesh with a sharp turn, and the power of their wings...my, they can blow the roof off a house with one mighty stroke," Gravon comments, a small smile kissing his lips as I imagine anyone riding a beast I am only familiar with in fairy tales. "Oh course, the age of those who tamed those creatures and would fly into parties on them, those days are long gone."

"People used to fly them to parties?" I am in awe at the thought of someone arrived at some masquerade dressed up in elegant attire having just hopped from a beast known for burning villages and stealing princesses. "I would think them more useful for battle."

The Duke nods, offering me his hand as there is a steep step to be climbed. Taking his hand, he helps me up the step, my eyes drifting to the King who still paces himself from us like before, not caring to tangle himself in our conversation. "Yes, they were ever so dangerous in battle, but dragons were also a sign of immense wealth as only the royals or warlords could afford to make the reigns to tame the beasts, daring to make such entrances all for the approval of the crowd. The age of those who fly upon the dragons is long gone, at least for two centuries. There are statues in the soldier's quarters of the King's palace of knights riding upon the dragons as they face armies." The way the Duke speaks of these days, it as if he is recalling some story that once inspired him. The spark in his eye resembles that of a child speechless at a sight so beautiful that it motivates them. The Duke talks of those who rode on dragons as if legends, those who made an impact, who were able to accomplish such an action to be remembered for centuries.

"It sounds amazing," I reply, the only way to describe the idea of people riding dragons. Would I like to try that? I would be a fool to say no but knowing that dragons are seen with a negative context, I would have to rethink it when taking in the likelihood of a dragon wanting to be strapped down after having run free for centuries. "And the King's mother, as the goddess of the dragons, I take it she has ridden one."

The Duke shrugs his shoulders. "Goddesses and gods are not known for their interactions in the realm of Iduna really, especially for allowing the common folk to witness their presence, but I would expect that-

"Why should Dregh's interactions with her creations be any of our concerns?" Kyril asks, placing his input into the conversation as he stops, waiting for us to catch up. His eyes are a bright blue, as if a sky without any clouds, a bright blue that seems to spark up the darkness surrounding him. "Dregh is simply a goddess who does not make time to impact our lives, so why should we concern our lives with the thoughts of what she has done or will do." He speaks of his mother as if someone he has little patience for, as someone he finds to be a chore to consider.

I know he found the woman that his father married to be the woman he called his mother, but he speaks of his actual mother as if she has no place in his heart sure. And yes, the gods and goddesses may have strong children like Kyril for game and bets, but it amazes me distant connection that these deities keep with their children. The moment Kyril's gaze meets my stare, I find myself taking in a shaky breath, my shoulders tensing as I try and think of something to switch the topic to. But I cannot simply change the subject when the woman we speak of is about to be in our presence. "As for what is to happen within the hour, Lady Candice," the King begins, taking a step towards me as I catch up, his presence looming over me.

"When you are spoken to by Dregh, you do not speak to her right way, but wait for my approval. When she looks to you, you will never look to her because your head will be bowed the entire time as you kneel to her. When she calls upon the crust of hell to break and allow the darkest monsters to roam free, you stay silent. You will carry none of that spirit that you do with me or anyone else. One word spoken out of line and she will not dare give you a second glance before turning you to ask and chaining your soul to an endless room of darkness."

That shuts me up from any quick response, fear entering my souls as I hear these rules that the King has just set forth. Do not even look at her? What would I imagine her to look like? Perhaps flaming red hair, black eyes, pale skin, and a cape that holds dragon scales, but I have never seen a goddess. I have no idea what standards to hold goddesses to for their appearances as I have never laid eyes upon one.

Maybe Dregh is one of the gods Soka said that her kind prayed to. I wonder who prays to Dregh and how many gods there are in this realm. I wonder how she made dragons, how she allowed herself to have children merely for entertainment and bets and wrapped herself up in a haven away from people. But most of all, I wonder why Kyril insists on my attendance when he visits his mother, why he wants me to stand before the goddess and pray that she does not strike me down. But I can understand why Kyril has eyes that glow different colors, resembling galaxies of the universe, oncoming storms to frighten his enemies, and how they hold some sort of power to them.

The eyes are the window to the soul, yet I cannot read his soul. "If I am to speak no words or draw no attention to myself, then why must I be present for this meeting?" I ask, the King's head looking down upon me, lips pressed together in a firm line as I hold my ground. It is a legit question.

Kyril takes wraps his fingers around my arm, gripping it tightly as I feel a sort of electric spark. It could be what he calls that mate bond, but it could also just be an electric shock-like feel seeing that he is half of a godly power. "The blood of a lamb." It sounds religious, like something you would find in a religious text, but the way Kyril says it, something tells me darker moments are head. "The blood of a lamb shall silence the wind and call upon the storm." My eyebrows knit together, my body moving back as I pull my arm from Kyril's hold, a tug at the corner of his lips occurring. "Now, let us go forth, for we are almost there."

Turning around, the King continues the hike, the Duke and I following in pursuit as the wind only draws stronger, making me wonder how the blood of a lamb can silence the wind that only seems to be growing more powerful. How could we even find a lamb here to slaughter, all the way up on this mountain. Do lambs even exist here? I would assume so since Kyril mentioned the name of the animal, but I do not know if he is saying something symbolic or is just going mad. As we only near the peak of the mountain, the clouds hold a darker tint, like a dark purple, the clouds swirling around the peak where I can make out the outline of some statue.

It looks like just a simple gray stone, a pillar with a sphere on top. With every step, the ground seems to become more unsteady, as if the dirt beneath our feet has begun to shift like the clouds. There are a few steps leading down to a circular cutout where the stone pillar is located, the dirt colored onyx black, the pillar holding symbols on the sides, my mind processing the symbols right as I read them. The peak we are on, it is called Dragon's Landing, giving a perfect name for meeting the goddess of dragons and fire. Kind of a cheesy name.

As for the rest of the symbols, they tell a story, a story of a child born from ashes and rising into a flame, wings sprouting from her back, a mighty stroke every time she flew that was able to snap the trunks of trees, and the crafting she begun that would soon transform into dragons the moment she breathed fire into their lungs and greed into their souls. If anything, Dregh is appearing scarier by the moment.

"So how do we call her?" I ask, turning to the Duke as he stands next to me, his face pale unlike before. His eyes hold fear, something I did not want to see as I wanted to rely on him for reassurance that this goddess is not as bad as she seems. After all, the last line of symbols on the pillar told of a battle where Dregh called upon her most loyal dragon, unleashing hell not just upon the army, but on women, children, and a strip of land that is cursed by her fire.

"How does the prey call its predator?" the Duke responds, meeting my gaze as my heart races in my chest.

"The prey does not call its predator," I reply, raising an eyebrow in confusion.

"That is where you are wrong, for the moment that the prey comes out of hiding the predator has picked up their scent. The moment the smell of prey reaches the predator, they are hooked."

Looking to the King who stands at the opposite side of the pillar, I watch as he takes out his sword, his eyes meeting mine as those orbs become darker than night. It is as if his stare holds me in a trance, every step he takes towards me only making me think of the lamb. A lamb is innocent, a graceful creature who follows their shepherd. A lamb has never killed. The moment that the King stands before me, his sword in hand, his free hand reaching out to grab mine, I pull away, taking a quick step back. "I am not a lamb," I state, my voice stern as the wind only picks up. "You still need me alive, my King, you still need me alive."

"And I will keep you alive, I just need the blood of a lamb. The innocent little female who would never dare harm another creature."

Reaching out again, he misses as I jump back, only for the back of my heel to hit one of the steps, my body falling backwards as the King acts fast. But I act faster. The moment he lunches for me, I roll over, clothes covered in the black dirt, rising to my feet as I grab the sword from the Duke before he can hide it from me. Lifting the sword, I hold it out, pointing at the King as he stands up, shaking his head. "It seems like you forget what I am. It is so strange that someone who seems so intelligent could be so forgetful."

The sword flies from my hand, right past the King as it lands in the dirt, far from reach. The King lifts his hand, flicking his wrist as the dirt moves beneath my feet, pulling me towards him. Right away I run, trying to head in the opposite direction, only for the dirt to move opposite of my direction at a faster speed. Like running up an escalator, I cannot do it, I cannot match or even increase my speed to get out of this trap, my lungs beginning to burn as I find myself only being pulled towards the King that awaits his prey. The moment my back feels a sharp edge pressed against it, the dirt stops moving and the King takes my left hand, raising it up to the sky. Taking the blade, he runs it across my palm, applying pressure as I hiss at the stringing pain, my eyes watering as I witness a trail of my own blood trickle down my arm. Instantly the King pulls me with him towards the pillar, placing my bloody hand on the sphere at the top, the cold stone only making the pain worse as I try and fight his hold, but as he lets go of me, the wind stops.

The blood of the lamb has silenced the wind, meaning that my predator has smelt my blood, calling it to me, and that the oncoming storm is near. As the clouds in the sky darker to black and a red lightning bolt hits the side of the mountain, I shriek, ducking for cover as the lightening seems to surround us. Looking to where the first strike hit, I see a fire growing from it, the flames white and blue, a shadow in the flames, the shadow taking the shape of a female. Dregh. And just as silence fills the mountain top, time standing still, and an atmosphere forms around me, one of fear and cowardice. The flames begin to die down, decreasing in size as they seem to be swallowed by the ground, slowly unveiling the goddess before us as I clutch my hand, blood running down my arm. "So, my latest creation has called upon his creator," a voice rings out, one that I do not know whether to call it beautiful or terrifying. She talks with a poise you would expect a proud and demanding ruler to possess, a sense of darkness lurking behind that tongue of hers. "Calling upon his creator with the blood of one so innocent to this realm, a species time has tried to forget."

Kyril takes my arm, pushing me down to my knees roughly, reminding me to follow the instruction that he gave just minutes ago. To bow my head, to not look to her, to not speak to her, and to show no sign of disrespect. Duke Gravon takes the same stance as me, bowing his head as he closes his eyes from the temptation to gaze upon the goddess. "Where did you find this little fox, a little girl who too holds a silver tongue." She has called me a fox, a creature both sly and selfish. "She is fresh to Iduna."

Kyril moves from me, his boots digging to the black dirt as I allow my eyes to remain open, focusing them on the ground as I dare not look to the goddess no matter how much I wish to. I am scared that she could turn me into ashes within my first sign of disrespect. "She came through a crack in space, mighty Dregh," Kyril responds to his mother, calling her what anyone else would. His own mother does not wish to be spoken to like she gave birth to him, no, for she only wanted to have him for the entertainment. Now her entertainment calls upon her for reasons I do not yet understand. Kyril decided to pay his mother a visit just days ago when I pushed his limits, not telling me why his mother would be useful to anything except remind me that he holds so much power that I should never think about angering him again. "I would have put her to sleep by now at the bottom of a river, but she holds so much value to the search for Heka."

I thought that the gods and goddesses did not concern themselves with the life down below, but if Dregh knows of my father and perhaps is involved with the search for him, then I am scared. If my father did go around slaughtering the children of these gods, then they would want revenge for the cost my father took from them. No, I doubt the gods would want to find my father for slaughtering their children for sentimental reasons that a parent should possess, but for the damage to their source of entertainment. "She can translate the words he writes upon stone and paper, can she?" Dregh asks, her voice getting closer as I realize that she is approaching me, a magnetic pull for my eyes to look to her only getting stronger. "You need her to track him better, a man that has the power to cloak himself from the gods. I take it that you do not fully trust a word that leaves her mouth."

A pair of feet come before me, where shoes would be on her feet is a layer of purple dust, dark purple as it seems to be in the pattern of scales, fading away the higher you look to her legs. Unlike anyone I have seen in this realm, her dress is different from what I can tell, a short train behind her of a dark gray dress, the fabric covering her mid-thigh and higher. As my eyes are tempted further upward, I can see the design of her attire, the long sleeves that drape around her wrists, dark green scales sewed into the material from the elbows and below. I remind myself to not look higher, lowering my head as the goddess takes a step around, beginning to circle me as I see smoke rising from every footprint she leaves. "She wishes to return back home, thus we cannot trust every word," Kyril confirms, clearing his throat as I can tell he is nervous.

"So why did you bring her here?"

Silence, the goddess finishing her circle around me as I am left looking back at her ankles where I can make out thin, white tattoos on the inner-side of her feet, patterns of circles that intersect, lines interwoven in the shapes, and dots along the center.

Sparks run through my body, my skin paling as I find my chin lifted, my eyes taking in every inch of the goddess as she leans down before me, looking right at me. The front of her dress is breathtaking, the gray material becoming scales the higher up, a low scoop in the front as her heart is on full display, dark purple, every twist of it shown as it seems to glow through her pale skin, like some illusion. A necklace around her neck holds a red stone with sharp edges, her black hair draped over her shoulders as it falls to her jagged collarbones, holding a wavy texture as I find my eyes moving further up her features. An oval face, high cheekbones, full and dark lips, eyebrows anyone would be jealous of, and those eyes...those eyes that hold every secret to the universe. She seems to hold all of space and time with one glance, dark colors swirling in her orbs as she takes in my appearance, scanning me over like some art critic. It is as if she is reading right into my naked soul, stripping me down to the basics of life.

A smile, one that makes my heart skip a beat in fear, tugs at her lips, her fingers releasing my chin as it feels a slight burn. Rather than walk away, she grabs my bloody arm, pulling me up to my feet as her fingers run over my cut palm, a glowing light appearing as the wound is healed. Looking over her shoulder to Kyril, she smiles, a laugh filling the dead air. "You did not bring her here just because she is a key to finding Heka, my dearest little son," Dregh begins, turning back to me as her hand cups my cheek, head tilting to the left. "No, you brought her here as if to gain some sort of relief or sense of pride. You think this little human to be your soul mate."

"My mother, that is not why I am here, I am here to offer you the missing puzzle piece to finding Heka," Kyril refutes, looking nervous as Dregh pulls me closer to her.

"You would protect her from anything, Kyril, and that is such a shame." A shame? What does she mean by it being a shame? "Because I have already read her past, her memories, her reasons, and the motivation that keeps her putting up with you and your blinded actions."

Dregh knows who I am. She knows that my father is that man that her and so many others are after.

"And my oh my, King Kyril of Iduna, is she the little most sly little fox of them all, an oncoming storm just around the corner...and you have no idea what she means."

Chapter 16

"You have no idea, do you, what she means to all of this, this hunt that you have placed so much concentration on," Dregh points out, turning to her creation as Kyril's lips are pressed together in a firm line. "You say she is merely a translator to your quest but have you no idea the symbol she bears on her soul." What does she mean? Does she know me to be the daughter of Heka? If she knows me to be the daughter of someone that the gods are too looking out for, then she would not hesitate to strike me down, but then again, Dregh seems like someone who loves to play a game. "So innocent you call her, so pure to this world of darkness, but that is merely her past."

I pull my eyes away from the goddess, seeing Duke Gravon with his head still bowed, knuckles white as his hands are fists upon the onyx dirt. He is straying his eyes from the goddess, looking towards me briefly as fear is mirrored in his eyes. His eyes show the same emotion my mother's did years ago when another well-known magician dared to do what my father did, but he did not know the fire he was playing with. I had attended the performance with my mother as it was a tribute to my father's passing, the elites of the entertainment industry surrounding us. That magician wound up in the hospital with internal bleeding, three broken ribs, and third-degree burns.

No magician could recreate my father did because that performance of my father's was not an illusion or cheap trick, but actual magic without any extra affects. Gravon holds the terror in his eyes my mother did when that magician almost met his end, an indescribable fear that only grows in power. From the way Kyril and Gravon talked of the gods, I can understand why being in the presence of a god could be so terrifying, but yet it seems like the fear Gravon holds in his eyes is all because of me, and not Dregh.

"Tell me, Candice, how did you happen to wind up realms away from your home?" The goddess looks to me, her head tilted to the side as my throat runs dry. "Look at that, my dearest son, how she is brewing up a lie to lace your mind with as it takes hold and makes you believe her."

"She is my mate," Kyril snaps at his mother, taking one swift stride to place himself directly between his mother and me. "I trust her more than I could ever trust you. You had me just to show off to the other gods, to use for your own selfish needs because eternity is boring."

A laugh fills the air, causing chills to run down my spine as I look past the King before me and to the goddess who is now entertained. "If that is your reason for trusting a human, Kyril of Iduna, then I certainly overestimated all the intellect in that head of yours, all that logic." Dregh walks forward, her footprints leaving trails of a shallow fire, her presence only coming closer to me one again as she is watching me like some piece of art from a museum, as if some piece of work to be admired. Why? I am human, a mere mortal and holding no power in my veins like someone worthy of this world filled with the unreal. "Do you not recall why Iduna was created, Kyril of Iduna, why the gods crafted this world for your kingdom to have existence?"

A force pulls me upwards, the goddess holding out her hand as she twists it, my body following her control as I stand before the goddess, head held high as she inspects me further. "The realm of Iduna was crafted to shield us from the monsters of flame, of hunters lurking in the darkness, and of the fear of our kind being wiped from existence," Kyril contributes to the conversation, bring back words Soka once told me, of how humans were the hunters of her kind and others, the reason for isolation in fear of extinction. To think these people of magic fear the existence of humans, a species holding no power like those from this realm. "The gods wanted a haven for their kin and crafted Iduna, a haven to protect us from the monsters of the light. But those hunters died centuries ago when the last dragon fell, no longer training their kin as they saw we had disappeared."

"Tell me then, Duke Gravon of the Rolling Mountains of the Eastern Isles, since you have studied the creation of this realm, of the unreal power these hunters possessed," Dregh commands, speaking out to the Duke who has remained silent in all of this.

The Duke rises to his feet, looking up to me, fear reflected in his eyes. "The strongest family of hunters, they were known for their adaption to our ways of fighting, learning of the magic we possessed. They stole from the elves and witches, creating stones and grains that were used to defend and protect their lives, that were used in magical spells that could hide you from your predator, and even as teleportation devices. This family found a way to bind these materials into powerful weapons and were the reason for why the elves became a race of darkness and hate," Duke Gravon explains, switching his gaze back to the goddess who holds me in her magical grasp.

"These people came from a land of sand and shallow trees. The mightiest warrior and hunter of their kin was called Heka of the Nile, a hunter who knew of the gods and goddess and that they had created Iduna. Heka of the Nile knew that the duty bestowed upon him was to silence the souls of the creatures of Iduna, so he worked on a way to reach the gates of Iduna and finish what his family had begun."

"And his head was cut from his shoulders by an elf, a beautiful elf who seduced him," Dregh adds, her eyes meeting mine as I am released from her hold, my feet stumbling back a little as the name hits me. Heka of the Nile. The name my father has taken and the Nile River in the name of that hunters, meaning he was from Egypt. My father spent much of his time in the Middle East, even focusing five years of his life to that country as he was constantly on digs there and making connections to find certain pieces for his work. Mother said that my father found his true potential in Egypt. "Heka of the Nile, his children lived on, passing down stories for their own children and soon enough, after the story of the world of Iduna was seen as a silly children's story, one of these children believed it to be true."

"So Heka, the one roaming Iduna right now, is a descendant of the original Heka who wished to destroy Iduna?" I ask, "What did this Heka of the Nile do?"

Kyril steps forward, eyes reflecting the fear that the Duke too holds. "He murdered a god, something that was thought no mortal could ever do." Kyril turns back to his mother, shaking his head. "What are you implying about Candice? That she is a hunter? That she is a relative of Heka of the Nile?" A smile pulls across Dregh's lips as she lifts her chin, shoulders rolling back.

"No, she is not here to murder us all, to slay us, no, for that is not why she has stepped foot in Iduna. She looks innocent, my dearest Kyril, like an innocent flower plucked from their home and in new territory. She is still learning of Iduna, taking it all in, and she does want to leave."

"What are you implying?" Kyril asks, voice stern as my throat dries.

The goddess lays a hand on my arm, sparks flying through my skin as smiles. "She was born to seduce any powerful being of Iduna, my son, to determine the fate of your very existence. And my, she will lead you to Heka, she will indeed."

"You do not know me," I snap to the goddess, my voice stern as the goddess pulls away, shocked at my lash out to her. "I just want to go home."

"And you are home," Dregh informs, her voice a mere whisper, as if to keep it away from the ears of Kyril of Gravon. She holds out her hands, a glossy bubble forming around us, sheltering our existence from that of Kyril and the Duke. "You have been gone for so long, Candice of the Nile, daughter of Heka, and descendant of Heka of the Nile. My, oh my, how the bloodline of the world's deadliest hunters has changed. You were born to return back to Iduna, to finish what your long-lost relative started. You came here to find your father, to hunt down the hunter of demi-gods." My jaw is clenched as the goddess smiles. "But your father merely hunts demi-gods, unable to truly take on the battle between a god and a mortal. He is not strong enough, but you, my dearest little Candice, hold such a strong loyalty to your flesh and blood, that you will soon pick up a sword and taint that soul of yours in crimson red."

"That is not true, I am not some murderer. I am here to find my father and return home," I refute, arguing with a goddess who could easily kill me. "Why not slice off my head already, make sure I never get the chance to murder a god?" I question, as if taunting the goddess as she takes a step back from me, taking in my appearance.

"Why would I end the game before it has even begun. I am sure you have heard of my reputation in the ring of gods, how I am feared most, how I love to play a game."

"I figured you liked to play games the second I heard of you," I reply, watching as the goddess flicks her wrist, golden mist circling her hand as her eyes glow gold."

"And you think yourself incapable of killing a god," Dregh points out. "I have feuds with gods and goddesses who have upset me for centuries. I know their weakness and their limits. I know what will happen to you when you find your father, how you will slay your first enemy before nightfall as you would do anything for family." Dregh flicks her wrist again, the golden mist in her hands forming the shapes of people, one holding a sword as they strike another down, the body turning into mist that falls to the ground we stand on. "You are part of a family whose loyalty was never underestimated. Stories of your bloodline still live on in Iduna, how one hunter took down an entire army just to find their sister, how one slayed a dragon to avenge their husband's death, and now, another child of Heka has emerged, to find her father lost in a world she will soon come to know as her duty to destroy."

"I have no need to destroy a world made of the unbelievable, for your world does nothing to my own. I wish to leave it as soon as possible. I will not become someone to be known for slaying gods and goddesses because that is impossible."

"And yet you thought that a world like Iduna was impossible," Dregh points out. "Soon enough, things will awaken within you, for Heka of the Nile did not just stone that helped give him a leverage to his hunt, but he stole the soul of a goddess, cutting it from her body before it could escape, allowing the soul to be consumed by his through a darker magic than any other, his bloodline carrying the soul of that goddess. That is the mark you bare upon your soul."

I find my heart races, the sound of drums banging in my head as a headache begins. "And what was this woman the goddess of?" I ask, looking back to Kyril and Duke Gravon who stand parallel to time.

Dregh smiles, opening up her palm as her flesh becomes crimson red on her hand, as if blood is covering her flesh. "The goddess of war."

The bubble surrounding us comes down, allowing for the King and Duke to become back into our conversation as I take in a shaky breath. "Soon enough, Kyril," Dregh begins, turning to her son, "you will not be protecting this female from Iduna, but you will find yourself under her as she takes your life from you."

Dregh goes up in flames, blue and white flames consuming her body as she fades away into the sky, the weather becoming a heavy rain as I am left alongside a King who thinks I am his soulmate and a Duke that fears me. They have been told I am to be feared, but Kyril does not believe that, not yet, not the way he looks at me like I am someone he has sworn to protect for all eternity. As the wind blows and the rain beings to soak my clothes, my head spins as thunder rolls in the distance. Dregh wants to play a game with me and she wants Kyril to be another piece of entertainment in it.

"She often says things to mess with your head," Kyril comments, as if trying to persuade himself that he does not believe what his mother has said. "We will return to the camp and head in the direction of Heka. Going to Dregh was just a waste of time and she took advantage of it," he includes, grabbing my arm, sparks flying through it as he holds me close, eyes staring into mine, the appearance of hopelessness shown in his eyes as they trace over every detail of my face. "She wants to pin me against my mate because her mate left her for a mortal back in the realm of humans." He holds me close, an arm wrapped around my waste as I want to push it away and run for the hills. Unlike him, I find myself accepting every word that Dregh told me, but that does not mean I believe every word that goddess spoke. I will not murderer. I will not taint my soul in crimson red. "We shall return you to the palace, to keep you safe from these darker places of Iduna." I shake my head.

"I am here to find Heka, to return home-

"Your home is here, with me!" Kyril shouts, the ground rumbling beneath my feet as my eyes widen and skin becomes pale. "Where my home is, so is yours."

"And if my home is with you, then I am to go with you on the hunt," I reply, taking his hand, squeezing it as I know what I must do to see my father. If Dregh was correct about my family being related to the line of a powerful family of hunters, then I am screwed. "I stand beside you." I know the words I must say, how to word my every phrase to make this male believe that I trust him and will be beside him as we find Heka. I may be insane, but I wish to return home, to see my mother, and to make my family once whole again, even if it means placing myself in terrible danger.

"You do?" Kyril asks, his free hand moving up to cup my face as my throat dries and become sore. He looks into my eyes with a sorrow matched with a sense of happiness or relief. He looks at me like how I would imagine my father to look at my mother when they are reunited after so many years of isolation from one another. He looks at me as if we have been in love for ages and have finally renewed the love we have for one another. "You will stand beside me?" He asks, coming in closer as his eyes begin to slowly shut, his lips only coming in closer.

"I will," I whisper, moving my lips closer to his as I know this is for my family, for my family to become whole once more. "Because we are mates," I add, giving Kyril false hope as we seal our conversation with a soft and short kiss, and as he holds me only closer, I find a darkness growing within my soul. A darkness uncontrollable and just waiting to be released.

Chapter 17

How do you kill a god or goddess?

That has been all my mind is focused on ever for two days ago, when Dregh surrounded me with her words that flowed from her silver tongue like a river. Kyril is right in the fact that you can never trust a word that his mother speaks; however, I am to never underestimate Dregh, as I know she loves a good old game. She wants to play a game of chess, but not one against me, no, but one against other gods. It was clear when she spoke to me, how she said she knew other deity's weakness and how to use them to her advantage.

My one question in her game of chess, is not which piece am I to her, but who is her opponent? If Dregh plans on using a human from the line of the strongest hunter, a human with no knowledge or ability to kill someone of her stature, then is this opponent that weak, or does she just want to play a game? With my mind wrapped around those thoughts, I completely disregard the conversation before me, as Kyril talks to his trackers, showing them a map and he points along different mountain ranges and bodies of water.

King Kyril of Iduna, a naive and weak king for his kingdom. Sure, before I saw him as some strong and mighty king, the way he conducted himself, how people talked of him, and hell, how my first impressions of him was him holding me over a balcony as I screamed. However, I see it now, I see his arrogance in a new light, his yearn for someone to belong beside him. Being King at a young age and having grown up in a palace where you have seen your father murdered, your mother never visiting because she is a goddess who gives no concern for you, and his only friend to be his mentor to teach him academics and battle skills, I see how that has made him appear weak to me now.

The king I once thought of as mighty and bold is nothing more than someone my age now, prone to being taken advantage of, someone so desperate for the company of someone their age that could offer them a simple slice of happiness, and someone I too will play just has his mother has played him.

Kyril does not believe Dregh because he always thinks she is to lie, to try and take a piece of his happiness from him, while in reality, he should have listened to the woman he detests. Dregh told me of a possible future, yet I wish to disprove her, to show her I will not murder, and to show that I will leave Iduna with my father. So, what if my relative was some mighty hunter, for he has been long dead and any fighting skill I have in me, Kyril has easily been able to disarm me. If I cannot even defeat a demi-god, then how can I defeat a god? I have been told that Heka has slayed many demi-gods, as if that his is goal here, but he made a mistake in slaying Kyril's father and not Kyril himself. If this is true, then I do not know the image I expected my father to have.

"Lady Candice?" My presence in the discussion around me is acknowledged once more, snapping me out of my thoughts as I sit before a group of men that overlook a map, their eyes locked on mine as my throat runs dry. "Did you not hear the plan?" Duke Gravon asks, his voice a tad shaken as it has been since the day on the mountain when I saw in his eyes a fear not caused by Dregh but caused by me. Ever since that day, Duke Gravon has tried to pull himself away from me, no longer someone for some friendly conversation, but someone who makes comments every now and then, avoiding me as much as possible. Why? He knows not of what Dregh said I could be capable of, but he knows that Dregh confided in me, treated me as if someone to associate herself with, and wished to see me again. That alone is enough to make him fear what assumes me to be capable of. All of Kyril's other men see me just as a mere human, seeing me as no threat as they only think that I am here to help their king find a man that has erased himself from the maps. "Our plan is to head out tomorrow morning, before the sun rises, and to head west into the Forest of Zella, taking a shortcut through there and then into the mountains Heka is said to be residing within."

"How long of a journey?" I ask, sitting up straight as I remember the golden eyes of Dregh the moment she told me I would murder my first enemy on the day that I am reunited with my father, before the sun can even set. But who would be my first enemy? It would have to be someone here from the camp, someone already plotting something against me, but who? Duke Gravon is a no, as he is too scared me of, plus, he knows his king is head over heels for me, meaning he would not dare threaten the life of the king's supposed mate. The king looks to me, his head probably filled with conflicting thoughts. He must be smart than how he is acting now, some part of him knowing that because his mother left with haunting words hanging in the air, I am more than just some human who came to Iduna on accident. Kyril believes that his mother was playing another game, trying to take some form of happiness from him.

What happens when he discovers who my father is? My father who has traveled around this realm, murdering the children of the gods, and here Kyril is, unaware that I am the daughter of the man he wishes to kill. Why do I hold such high loyalty to a man who I barely know, who perhaps has murdered so many like what I have heard? He is family, flesh and blood that has been missing from my life for years. It is not just loyalty alone that keeps me persistent on finding my father, but the fact that I want to know why he never returned home to mother and me, why he spent so much of his life trying to leave his perfect life back home behind for one of a lone traveler seen as an enemy or a demon. A sense of curiosity aids my determination to find my father, not to mention he may hold the key to return back home.

"The forest is a day's ride, then we rely on the gods to guide us to Heka," Duke Gravon responds, his voice shaky, already knowing to believe in the warning Dregh gave. Was he right to fear that warning from Dregh? He believes her words to be set in stone, but that kind of fate Dregh believes is mine, it cannot be right. Dregh does not know me, does not know who I am and is only basing her believes off the character of my father. "There is a tribe of elves within the forest, perhaps even helping to protect Heka."

"Why would elves try and protect Heka?" I ask, turning to Kyril as he takes from the table a goblet, running his fingers around the gold rim, eyes glowing bright gold. A golden mist comes from the goblet, expanding into the air as the king looks bored, as if this magic that he is capable of does not fascinate him.

One of the men in the room beside Duke Gravon steps forth, opening his mouth as he forms his reply. "There are those in this realm that have sold their souls to the belief that the gods should pass away, that the realm is better off without supreme beings running things from afar." The more I listen to this, the more I wonder how complex the inner-workings of this realm are. Beliefs, the morals, religions, the deities, and even the governments here, I truly wonder how this world compares to my own. "Heka has been slaying children of the gods for years here, but he does not yet have the power to go against a god." My father, a man that has spent so much of his life perfecting his magic, slaying the children of gods, and hiding away, has not believed himself to be strong enough to kill a god, much less fight one. However, even with all these facts, Dregh believes me capable of slaying a god when my father has been practicing longer than me and cannot even try his skills against a god. How can Dregh be so sure about what my supposed fate is to be?

"And what happens when we find Heka? When we find the elves? Will we not be fought against?" I ask, seeing that every man here has a sword, or some form of weapon held by their side, but I have no way to protect myself. I cannot be kept from the battle if these men plan on murdering my father, I must be there. I have to be there to make sure that my father and the only man that holds the key to getting out of this world does not die.

Kyril nods, placing the goblet down as he points to a map, one where a forest is marked out. "The leader of the tribe is not too keen on my race, Lady Candice, but she does enjoy a good human, especially a female since she has not set her eyes upon one in centuries."

"And when we find Heka?" I question, getting ready for the words that will make my head race with thoughts and a sense of duty fall upon me.

Duke Gravon takes in a deep breath, knowing the words that must be spoken before we head out for the elves. "When we find Heka, Lady Candice," he begins, placing his hands upon the table, "then justice will lie within the hands of the one who holds the sword."

By sunrise my horse is saddled up for the journey, the cloak placed around my shoulders, wind blowing, and my eyes sore from the sunlight that extending out upon the land. A soldier hands me the reins to the horse, my eyes looking past the individual as they interlock with the eyes of the king, his lips pressed firmly together as I wonder what the day ahead has not for us, but for me. It is as if we stand against one another now, knowing that this moment is one we have been waiting for if Heka is there today. Though just hours ago Kyril thought his mother to be speaking lies, but now he knows that we are close to the man we have both been trying to find. I am to be a loose cannon, unsure of how well I will be able to control myself the moment I set eyes upon my father once more. But just as I am a loose cannon, so is King Kyril, bloodthirsty and obsessed with revenge that he could become my biggest threat today.

The moment I get onto the horse and find myself nervous for the next few hours, the king only follows in mounting his own horse, ready to lead his men into a forest filled with elves that perhaps protect my father. As the crowd of horses become rowdy and the king leads the way, I no longer find myself beside him as usually, but rather pushed back in the middle of those just obeying the orders of their king. With their swords, bows, arrows, and axes tucked away and ready to be used if necessary, I find the need to grab one and keep it as my own for later only growing within. If I am to meet some elven ruler and there is to be some siege underway, I find it necessary to keep something pointy by my side to live another day.

By the time the sun is halfway up in the sky and a forest that stretches long and wide to a mountain range filled with ice and snow, I know that the moment to find my father is only approaching. My heart racing faster than a humming bird and my head spinning, my nerves only pick up as our destination becomes closer. Looking over the forest below, I can see a small stretch of white marble structures, running between a group of trees with slightly darker shaded leaves than the rest. Even in winter the tress have not lost their green hues, untouched by the snow just meters away from the territory of trees. In this world of the unreal and everything a child could read in any bedtime story. To think I have spent all my time within this realm on no break, constantly having my arm twisted as I wonder where the next day shall take me. If my father is there today and I watch him die, I know that Kyril will not let me go, but I also know that I will not go easy on any of them. Hell, I would try as hard as humanly possible to get out of here, to find my freedom and either seek a way back home or some form of haven as I live my life out here in this world. But if my father does not die today and I find myself beside him, I swear our mission will be to return home, to rebuild the family we once had. No, I will not spend the rest of my years within this realm, hunting down gods and goddess, playing Dregh's games.

"Lady Candice," a voice calls out, turning my attention over to the individual as I see Duke Gravon there, skin pale, and before the dark forest ahead as our horses come to a stop. "The King wishes for you to venture with him into the forest beside him." As my horse comes to a stop and I am helped by a soldier off my horse, the forest stands tall before us, causing me to feel miniscule.

"Thank you, Duke Gravon," I reply, knowing that the Duke is just scared of me, of what someone says I am capable of. Looking to the king who stands before a small path made by the trees, I know that he too has many questions spiraling through his mind. "My King," I speak out, walking over to the male who seems lost before the mighty forest ahead. "You wish for me to walk beside you." The King nods, not even turning his head to look my way.

"We should be to the tribe before sunset," the King announces to his men, turning to face them as he almost reaches out for me, fingers almost grasping my hand, only to brush past as he reminds himself what is about to happen. "Keep your swords close and your guard up at all times, for the elves are sly creatures, sly as foxes."

Turning around, Kyril faces the forest, looking at me through the corner of his eyes as I see his eyes dull for once, in a state I have never seen before. With his first step taken and my eyes focused to the forest ahead, I only follow him in pursuit, the men behind us not daring hesitate as the smell of dirt and sound of birds chirping seems so rare to me. The path before us is narrow, vines from the trees overlapping the stone path along the way, trees shading the forest floor as I look through the forest, to the strange plants growing within. Flowers grown up the trees, shades of light pink and orange, as if a vine as they only make the forest more beautiful. As we walk further in, birds fly above in the trees, bright blue wings and long beaks, their little bodies perched upon branches where small mushrooms grow upside down. For most of the journey in, we walk beside a small river, one with crystal blue water, silver fish swimming with the current, jumping in and out like a dolphin would in the ocean. If anything from this forest, it is far more stunning than any other portion of Iduna I have seen. Just as one of the men behind me begins to hum a tune, soon enough many of the other men have joined him, filling the silence with some song. A song about a dragon, one that had sacrificed itself for the king who he had sworn to protect. They sing of a dragon not having caused destruction as I would expect, but one who helped the land and dedicated its life to the safety of a single man.

"Tell me, Lady Candice, does your world hold any stories of dragons?" Kyril asks, drawing my attention away from the song and to the man that walks before me. "Stories that go back centuries ago about the mighty and scaled beasts who breathed fire."

So practically anything about a damsel in distress who was saved by some dashing prince from the dragon's layer or the mighty tale of Beowulf who died fighting the dragon. "Just stories mostly told to children now. Dragons who terrorized a village or stole some princess from her home. Nothing too memorable," I reply, pulling the cloak around my body closer in as a warm breeze brushes past. "Most stories now are about different types of futures that hold nothing pure and good in them." It is true, for most stories now read back home are about dystopian societies or themes that warn people from technology.

"Sounds like a home with no sense of imagination or history," Kyril comments, briefly looking over his shoulder to me, his eyes holding a hollow emotion. Looking back to the path ahead, he suddenly stops, holding up his hand as his men also stop, grabbing onto their weapons as they become worried. Looking to the men behind me, they are still, eyes scanning the forest floor as I look out into the trees, only, I do not see some beast or creature to be frightened of, but a woman dressed in a pale blue dress.

"King Kyril," the woman greets, a small distance away as her words feel soft and welcoming, a small smile tugging at her lips, and her gray eyes falling upon me. "The High One has been expecting your passage since sunrise." The High One? Is that the name of their ruler?

"As we have been on our way to greet the High One," Kyril replies, talking with a respectful tone, watching as the woman draws closer. She is an elf, her ears pointed at the top, a thin silver crown placed upon her head that holds emeralds on the bottom rim, her black hair pushed behind her shoulders, and her skin seeming to illuminate like the moonlight as she comes closer.

The elf stands before us now, tall, as tall as the King as she overlooks even the men in this group. As her eyes scan the crowd, they almost go past me as I am the shortest of the bunch, but the moment her eyes land on me, they stay put, widening she tries to hide a shocked facial expression. "What a peculiar creature to have by your side, King Kyril. The High One will be very intrigued by this." Because I am human. That must be why, because my father has been hidden by these people. "Tell me, King Kyril, why do you carry so many weapons with you?"

"We are traveling to the mountain, to train the new palace guards. We are passing through the forest to save time," Kyril responds rather quick. "We are requesting shelter for the night within the halls of your High One."

The elf smirks, looking smug as she keeps her eyes locked on me. "One would be unwise to withhold the wish of their king," she responds, taking her eyes off me and back to Kyril. "I shall take you to the palace as the Holy One has been expecting you and your guest."

"Then remember, elf, that she is my guest and not a gift to your ruler."

"We are simple creatures, my King," the elf explains, "never wishing to upset our lord." The way she talks, how she says her words, the elves know. They know what we have come for, and what Kyril's endgame is. They know we are here for Heka and they also know that I am human, meaning that they would have told my father. I may not know elves, but if these people have been sheltering my father for years then they would inform him that another human has entered their forest. My father already thinks that it is not me that has entered Iduna, but my mother, meaning he expects to see my mother when all of this is over, not the daughter he left ages ago.

"Then lead the way," Kyril instructs, the elf turning around, everyone following in pursuit as I feel myself becoming anxious. With the path being led by an elf and all the men around me positioning their hands close to their weapons, I find the need for a weapon in my hands only increasing with every step. As a child I was always told about elves in story books, about this wisdom, their kindness, and the special powers they possessed to help make the world beautiful. But these elves are not those from the books I read as a child. I remember calling Soka an elf back many nights ago, only for her to take it as a direct insult and warn me of the disintegrating morals of those who always seem so pristine. But as I watch this elf, as I have heard this elf speak, I find myself not wanting to get out of the reach of Kyril, but of the elves instead. Something is going to happen today, before the sun can even set, and I can only pray that I do not find myself becoming the person who Dregh said I would.

Chapter 18

Golden vines wrap around black, marble pillars, rising high to the ceiling where the glass roof allows the gray sky above to be put on display. The dark hall stretches not too far, the size of the hall nothing compared to Kyril's throne room, as this is a palace which is home to a small population of the subjects within the King's realm. The walls are a white stone, stain glass windows holding every shade of blue as they portray the running of water, dark blue fish swimming within, and a war upon the water.

The pillars run in two rows parallel to the other, leading up to a humbler throne, a throne woven from white roots, behind the throne a massive window that looks out to the river that runs behind the structure, small houses built on the other side as a wooden bridge leads to them. Around the room are different entrances to halls, either stairs leading up or halls leading further into the building as I wonder if my father is down one of the paths.

Standing beside the king, I can sense how tense he is, how stressed, and I know that although he does not keep his hands close to his sword, he has magic running through his veins. If a fight must occur, I should choose to stay beside him, as he will use his magic and I can easily take hold of his sword, but if he turns his magic on me I am out of luck.

"My King, the High One will be with us shortly," the elf that led us here announces as the doors we came from shut behind us, all the men on this journey standing in the hall as we await the elven ruler. With my heart beating fast and I find myself on edge, my eyes scan the hall over and over, looking to the doorways in case I catch sight of my father.

The elven women leaves us along in the hall, swallowed in the shadows of the hallway she enters, leaving us to the silence of the room. "It is a truly interesting story how this elven ruler gained her title," Kyril disrupts the silence, turning to me as he tries to make conversation. "The battle she fought five decades ago when she was just finding herself, that battle marked her out as a force to be reckoned with."

"What did she do?" I ask, knowing a conversation will help calm me down, to take my mind off my father.

Kyril looks to the throne, eyes swirling with a dark green color, a silver ring created around his pupil. "A dragon had attacked the mountains we just traveled over, her tribe fighting against a swarm of goblins whose ruler had trained a dragon years back. Her brother had fallen in battle beside her, body turned to white ash as he was scorched by the beast. When the dragon landed and was to bite the head off the elven ruler at the time, she took her axe and chopped off its head in one swing. She trapped the dragon's soul in a locket. Dragon souls require a dark magic to trap, but many have tried to do so because when you trap the soul of the dragon, you can feed off the strength they once had, allowing you to live longer, to even become stronger."

"So, because she trapped the soul of the dragon she has become feared by many?" I ask, the men around us listening in.

"No, not just that, Lady Candice," Kyril informs. "It takes a certain person to use that soul to help them live longer and become more powerful, but it takes a dark soul to craft that dragon soul into a weapon they use to destroy even the innocent." I raise an eyebrow, hoping he will elaborate on what exactly this elven woman did. Kyril leans in, face close to mine, a storm of gray and dark blue swirling in his eyes. "She killed a god with it, trying to capture that god's soul as well, but because the magic she used was so powerful, it destroyed the god's soul before it could even escape his body."

Duke Gravon looks to me, an expression of fear all because of me. "It is one thing to kill a god, Lady Candice, but it is another to destroy their soul."

Footsteps echo in the hall, coming closer as Kyril's men get to their knees, bowing their heads as the King stands still. As the footsteps draw even closer, I find myself following Duke Gravon as he gets to his knees, wanting to show respect for this woman. She killed a god because of the dragon soul she absorbed. If my relative absorbed the soul of a god, his power would have been even greater compared to this elf's.

"What a beautiful creature you have beside you, my King," a voice announces, one that sounds stern, overflowing with authority. I find myself looking over my shoulder, only to be surprised when I see right behind me the elf I was just informed on her power. Her dress is unlike many women I have seen here, how a split runs up the left side of her dark blue dress. The slit reveals a slender and long leg, only, it holds what appears to be massive scars from a giant creature. Perhaps the dragon she slayed many years ago, as the scars are hard to take my eyes off, looking like more pain I have ever felt in my life. As my eyes travel up her figure, I see her chest, how her dress scoops down to reveal a flat chest and a bronze locket in the shape of a diamond. The skin around the locket looks like green scales, as if slowly spreading across her chest, the tips of her fingers turning a dark green as her fingers hold several silver rings. "A female human, something time has forgotten. Women are the deadliest of creatures and yet you trust one beside you," the elf comments, fingers fidgeting suddenly as the elf reaches out to touch me.

Kyril grabs her hand, knuckles turning white from how tight his fingers are locked around her wrist, wanting her to not touch me. "She is not to be tainted by you," he snaps, releasing the elf's hand, warning her. The elf looks back to me, her eyes a dark orange, pupils not circular, but oval like a dragon's, what appears to be bags under her eyes are actually a set of dim blue scales just let the set on her chest. So, this is what happens when you trap and use the soul of a dragon, how it too absorbs you, creating one soul out of two. "She is not a gift, she is my mate."

The elf smiles, lips pulling back to reveal a set of pearly whites, but her back teeth are sharper than most, taking on the frightening teeth of a dragon. "What a shame such an innocent creature to be the one you are mated to, she deserves so much better."

"You dare disrespect your King?" Kyril growls, the walls shaking as the elven women offers a small laugh, as if trying to ease the King. "You know better than that, Lucretia, to try and disrespect your king." The elf looks back to me, her dark brown hair braided to the side, her ears not like the rest of her kin. Sure, they are pointy, but they turn a burnt red at the ends, golden piercings set at the ends, and just above her ears lays a silver crown that fits her head, emeralds running along the top as sapphires run along the bottom. "My men and I are passing through the forest to the mountains. They are training to become guards and we are seeking shelter for the night."

Lucretia nods, walking past me as her dress trails behind her, and from the back, there is no sign of any dragon features as she looks just as anyone else I have seen. "I have already made room for you and your men within the gathering hall, cots laid out for those who travel beside you. After all, I have expecting you since sunrise, my lord," Lucretia responds, looking over her shoulder to me, eyes meeting mine as chills run down my back. I am not a fan of the look she offers me. "I have set yours up within one of the guest rooms, my King, and for your human friend, I have prepared her a room in the same location." Lucretia turns back to face us, taking a seat upon her throne as her eyes scan me over, not looking me over like many have that I have met, but she looks at me like Dregh did, as if seeing right into my soul. Her eyes seem to darken the further she looks to me, as if reflecting what she sees. "But you must join us for our evening meal before the sun descents."

Kyril rolls back his shoulders, reaching his hand out for me to take, telling me stand on up. Reaching up, I take his hand which swallows mine, aiding me up to my feet as I am allowed to stand before the High One. What feels like electricity sparks between us as our skin comes into contact, it seems to pull us closer, beyond a simple gesture that lasts just seconds. The moment my hand slips away from his, the sparks are gone, just remains left over as they fade away as they climb up my arms. "We will join you for the evening meal, Lucretia, but before the sun can rise in the morning we will have to be leaving." With my mind wrapped around where my father could be here, as a conversation starts up again, my eyes wander off to the hallways, trying to see if someone is watching from the distance.

A hand takes hold of my arm, pulling me back to the conversation surrounding me as I see Duke Gravon and the rest of the men are back to their feet, Lucretia sitting down upon her throne, legs crossed as her slit reveals even more of the scar upon her flesh. Elbows set upon the armrests of the chair, she rests her chin upon her fingers, thumb brushing over her chin as she keeps her eyes focused upon me. She is not just interested in me, no, she does not look at me just because she is wondering what a female human is like, but she looks at me as if trying to figure me out, try and predict my next move. She does not see me as many I have met, how they assume me to just be someone who stands beside the king and offers him some pretty face or companionship. She looks at me as if she thinks me of more importance than the king of her land, as if I hold more respect than the man who wears a crown. She knows who I am, what I can do according to what she has seen my father do. They way she looks at me only establishes more proof that my father has committed the acts I fear are true of him.

"Then we shall take you up on that offer," Kyril finishes off the conversation, taking me with him to a hallway Lucretia conduct him towards. Kyril's men follow us, not looking to the elf whose skin has become consumed by the scales of the dragon she ended. We are led from the throne room, down a hallway to the left as silence fills the air. Kyril leads us into another room, one with open space and a small group of several elves, each turning their heads as their King leads his men through the place they call home. They seem tense as we pass by, stopping their discussion as we briefly remain in the open room, their eyes glued to the weapons with us.

Within the next few minutes the same elf that greeted us in the forest stands before Kyril, informing us she is to help me to my room as him and his men are led to their corridors. She explains that the women are separates from the men in this community unless bound in a ceremony which sounds like marriage to me. Separated from the men I have spent the majority of my time in Iduna around, I find myself alone with the elven women, led up a staircase and down a hallway. The walls of this hallway are higher now, the windows wider too as they overlook the river below, and a balcony perched over the widest area of the river. There she stands, Lucretia, hands placed on the balcony railing, and as the sunlight shines down upon her through the trees, the scales of her skin becoming more evident under the light. She is awaiting me, wanting to be around me without Kyril to interrupt every second.

"The High One has requested a private discussion with you," the elf informs, taking me right to the balcony doors as Lucretia stands just outside, her locket not around her neck, but the chain wrapped around her middle finger, the locket dangling as it shines under the sunlight barely present. "Go."

And go I do, walking onto the balcony as Lucretia gives me a soft nod, having me stand beside her. Placing my hands upon the railing just like the elf, she holds out her hand to me, the locket held out as well. I raise an eyebrow, holding out my hand as she drops the locket into my palm, motioning for me to take a look, to perhaps even open it. The cold metal is in my palm, the chain feeling heavier than it appears, my fingers brushing across the top of the locket. "You remind me of a man who once told me of his mission within this realm, how it fit right along with a belief we elves have held for ages," Lucretia informs, leaning her back against the railing as she takes a lot at her hands. "He told his name, of who he was related to." Lucretia smiles, placing her hand down as she lifts her heels off the floor and leans her head back to look at the sky. "I met that man once, before I had ever fought in battle. I was a child then, before the worlds had separated and Iduna was crafted."

"You met Heka, the one from the Nile?" I ask, one of my fingernails fitting right into the slot to open the locket.

"We elves take much time to age to our adult form, to become a warrior only means more than a century of age and wisdom must have been earned by us. It was so long ago when I met the man who held the gods in constant fear." I look back to the locket, wondering the appropriate moment to open it up and see what it inside. "I watched the battle the day the goddess fell from the sky, a mere mortal taking her down, and as I watched him as he carved her soul out, trapping that soul within his blood."

"So, he became the reason why you trapped the soul of that dragon?" I ask, finding the desire to open the locket and see what belongs within.

"I saw the power he absorbed, but I also saw the weakness he had the night he was murdered. The moment Heka of the Nile passed, I watched his children hold the blood with the goddess's soul, but by the time they tried to seek revenge, the realm had been made and closed off to the human race." Lucretia motions for me to open the locket now, my fingernail pulling on the locket as it clicks open. As I expect to find some sort of dark magic swirling within the locket, what I find is a simple locket, hallow as nothing comes out. "I captured the dragon's soul within the locket, afraid to absorb it right away as that kind of power could drive one insane with pain. Overtime I allowed the soul of the beast to feed into my body, into my soul, and you can see the evidence of that, on my skin, in my eyes."

Closing the locket, I find myself handing over the locket to Lucretia. "You speak of this to me because you know who I am already." Lucretia nods, taking her locket back, securing it back around her neck as the scales on her chest seem to shimmer. "Is Heka here?"

She pushes off the railing, heading back indoors as I get the cue to follow her, trying hard to not step on the train of her dress. "He has come and gone from this tribe for quite some time, a man who strikes fear into the King himself." Lucretia leads me into what appears as some mighty ballroom, a dome for the ceiling as it contains a beautiful oil painting of the night sky, constellations set up just as I recall from my astronomy class back in high school. The exam same constellation structure like back home as I have already discovered. It gives me hope when I look to the night sky these days and see the exact same layout of the stars. "Heka and I have a treaty, Lady Candice, one that keeps us elves as an ally of his as well as help cover his tracks."

"And Heka only plans on exterminating the children of the gods. What happens when he passes away and these children still are around?" I ask, Lucretia leading me towards the center of the room, a balcony at the far wall which overlooks what is the throne room. "These children will continue to be born unless the gods are killed off, and the gods are not easy to kill off."

Lucretia paces herself, walking in a wide circle around me, eyes trailing down my figure as she takes in my shape. "You think me to just speak of secrecy when you surround yourself with my enemy?" So Kyril is her enemy. It makes sense, as she knows him to be a demi-god, a child of a god which she may wish to take down.

"You have told me that Heka comes here and you are an ally of his. You have told me more than enough to land yourself as a traitor and dead at the hands of the king. Besides, you know what and who I am," I state, pointing out the obvious that she has already told me secret information that could get her killed.

"What you are is human and who you are is a child who has not yet realized her strength."

"I am not here to shed blood, but to find my father," I snap, "I am not going to find myself shoving a sword through someone's chest." Lucretia raises her chin, eyes hardening, and the scales upon her face seeming to spread.

"You think your father who has been missing from your life for so long and never thought of returning home will suddenly drop his destiny all for his precious little girl?" Lucretia asks, tone harsh as she clasps her hands behind her back. "He had so many years to go back to you, but he stayed here, knowing what had to be done." I shake my head. "You know this, but you are too blinded by a childish hope to come to your senses and accept the reality around you."

My eyebrows pull together, my lips pressed into a firm line. "Then you must also know that my blood line has a history of being loyal to family."

Lucretia shakes her head, laughing slightly as she does so, the tension only growing within the room. "Loyal to family, yes, but not as you think. They are loyal to the family cause, not to family alone.

The loyalty to one another is only because of their loyalty to their goal." I shake my head, not enjoying the fact that as this elf talks more, her eyes only seem to glow. "You are just a coward to accept the fact your father will not come back. You are not here to find your father and bring him back, Lady Candice, but you are here because of a darkness still asleep within you."

"Where is my father?" I ask, voice stern and commanding, a certain strength added to my voice that I have never felt before. My chest rising and falling heavy, my shoulders begin to tense as I just want to force the answer out of her.

The corner of the elf's lips pull upward, revealing those pointy teeth, her answer so close to being freed. "He will be joining us for dinner, Lady Candice, to fix a mistake he made long ago." Bloodshed. "A mistake that has lived on long enough."

Kyril. My father plans on killing Kyril tonight to fix the mistake of killing Kyril's father years ago. Like I said before, I am a loose cannon today, and I have no idea what I will do.

Chapter 19

The sun looks beautiful, just barely able to be seen as the trees clutter the sky. With my skin feeling the warm rays of the sun, a soft breeze blows as well, reminding me of the mountaintop where Dregh told me things I hope never come true. With my body leaning against the doorway of the balcony located at the highest tower n Lucretia's palace, I look out to the mountain range beyond the trees, where Kyril told the elves we were headed.

The mountains do not look like any other I have seen before, the tops covered in snow and black rocks, a frozen waterfall in the distances as the ruins of some old castle can be seen, the once white bricks holding a black strain as if a fire consumed the building. The trees are still green there at the base of the mountain, a set of stairs leading up to the road where the castle lays, but beyond the castle is the rest of the mountains that look unwelcoming and dangerous.

Millions of questions run through my mind, my thoughts consumed by what Lucretia told me just hours ago, on how my father plans to be a surprise guest for dinner who will try and kill Kyril. I remember the first time I heard of my father slaying someone, how

I told myself that could never be true, but as the nights pass and I hear more of what my father has done, I begin to wonder why I have come for him. Why did I come to Iduna in the first place? I recall being upset, my mother distant as always, and having enough of the life I was living. Never before had I thought that mirror in my father's office could do anything, just thinking my mother kept it around as a reminder of him.

Perhaps a piece of me had hope that my father was still out there, escaping into a new world through that mirror, and living an exciting life that made him excited to get up in the morning. I was tired of the same routine of a distant mother, friends who held more pity for me than true friendship, and a boyfriend who refused to agree with me even on the simple things. Maybe I even thought that if I could find my father and bring him back home...things would go back to the way they used to be: mother smiling, holidays celebrated with joy, a sense of belonging, and feeling that I would be actually loved for one. It is silly now, how my reasons for coming here were so damn selfish and I now find myself wondering if it was even worth it for me to come here.

My father is a murderer, murdering not just demigods who are Kyril's age, but also children no older than five. To think he may do this all because of some ancient family practice or destiny that he seeks to fulfill. Did mother know about this, about his reasons for coming here? I have always done so much for people, not just family, but friends and people I wanted to make an impression on as well. I put myself through so much worry and misery that I did not notice that I was burning bridges rather than building them. I constantly allowed my mother to go on her trips without any argument because I did not want to upset her and knew she was doing this all for our family. For friends I always stood up for them, always making sure they felt safe and like they could be themselves. I have always been loyal to those I want to keep in my life, to those who mean something to me.

But look where that loyalty has landed me now, tied up in a mess bigger than myself and lives on the line. My father is just protecting some family destiny, trying to take care of business, but even if he kills Kyril tonight he will not return home. My father will never come home, and I know this to be fact now, feeling so stupid for not accepting that truth before. Why do I even bother going along now, trying to find him, to think that he would help me return home? Then again, my options are limited because I am a human in a ream like no other and friends here are scarce. It is sad because Kyril is the only one here I could even call something close to a friend. He thinks me to be some soulmate of his and I know I feel no romantic connection to him, but I cans sense that we could become not just allies, but perhaps friends if under different circumstances. Would I be willing to watch him die tonight all because I need to have my father give me a way back home or whatever I seek from my father, or would I be willing to save someone who I may be becoming loyal to? Loyal to Kyril, someone who destroyed the portal back to my home, who I have held a sword up to and fought, and who even held me over a balcony the day we met. Kyril, someone who may just lash out at me if he knew I was Heka's daughter.

Turning back to the room before me, I walk towards the silver chest located in front of the bed, the room around me truly beautiful as Lucretia told me that it was designed by the previous High One's wife. The trunk is not mine for it come with the room, but when Lucretia dropped me off here, she told me to open the chest before dinner. She told me I would need the objects within the chest to make sure I survive the night if things go wrong. She expects a fight to break out tonight once my father kills Kyril, she expects me to say nothing to the King until it is too late.

My hands grabbing the handles and pulling the chest open, I am not met with what I thought would be weapons or some sort of potions, but rather a beautiful dress made of a navy fabric. I raise an eyebrow, lifting the dress as I examine it, wondering why she would want me to have this dress with me to protect me. It is a silly dress. As I pull the dress out of the chest, the sound of metal hitting the floor causes my body to freeze and my eyes snap to the floor, a smile spreading across my face.

Picking up the short sword, the metal is cold, the sword light, and the blade polished and sharpened. It is your simple design for a sword, nothing fancy, a silver handle with black leather around it, the blade ready to be used, and easy to swing. Lucretia hid the sword in the dress, but why hide it? Laying the dress onto the bed, I examine it, looking closer to the navy material as something catches my eyes. The inner material is not the same expensive fabric as the exterior of the dress, but a thick material. It does not feel rough on my skin or would be uncomfortable to wear, but I can tell it is a dress made for reducing the impact of any hit. Lucretia expects me to fight tonight, to draw blood, expecting me to partake in the actions Dregh said I would as well. If there is one thing I have seen in these two women who hold high power, they have both consumed pieces of a dragon. Although, it makes sense for Dregh to have scales on her body, or for her heart to been seen with every beat it takes, but not for Lucretia. Lucretia consumed the soul of a dragon, and it looks like the dragon has consumed her flesh in return, the scales upon her body being something that rubs me the wrong way. It makes me wonder what could happen to someone who becomes powerful, who takes another being's soul. Did Heka of the Nile, my great ancestor, face these mutations of the flesh, for he did consume the soul of a goddess?

Sliding my clothes off my body, I fold them up, setting them upon the bed as I look to the dress before me. It looks itchy, the material reminding me of the uniform I would wear when I did fencing. I take the dress, stepping into it as I look at my appearance in the mirror before me, my hair cascading over my shoulders as the navy material fits snug around my torso and chest. A modest front and back, it holds elegant silver embroidery at the sleeves and along the part that sweeps the floor. A silver fabric wraps around my torso like a belt, only adding to the appearance as I wonder where to place the dagger. My leg seems the most obvious placement, find a strap and just hold it there until needed. Though it may not be the best for the fastest gabbing time, it offers the most coverage for no one to see. Taking the sword, I hold it to the fabric of my previous attire, cutting a strip of fabric off as I pull my dress up, wrapping it around my thigh as my nerves only skyrocket with every breath I take. To think this is the day that I see my father after so many years of him being gone, on a day he tries to murder someone.

A knock at my door and I rush with my hair, a simple braid holding it all back as I head for the door, knowing this knock means that it is time to head to dinner. Pulling open the door and taking in a shaky breath, I am met with eyes holding every nebula within them, taking my breath away as the colors are vibrant and swirling around.

"I take it you were not expecting to see me calling you down for the evening meal," Kyril comments, eyes running over my figure. "You look mesmerizing, just as beautiful as the day you stepped into my palace." They can smell a traitor from miles away, the words of my father's journal entries back in the Temple swarming through my head. Kyril trusts me, yet something is off still with how much trust he has placed in me since his mother spoke with me. Dregh warned him of me, of what I could do, and what lays on the lie with me in his circle of those he trusts. He cannot be as dumb as he seems right now, how he still allows me in on his plans.

Looking back to my room, I see the sun has not even begun to set yet, still in the sky as the clouds hang low. "It seems early for dinner to start just yet," I state, finding myself backing away from the King as my father's words are echoed in my head. "Do the elves favor an earlier meal time?"

Without warning I find myself pushed into my room, feet stumbling back as I am caught by the small lounge chair that faces a fireplace. Landing myself into the chair, I watch as Kyril shuts the door behind us, trapping me in with him as I am ready to grab the small sword pressed up against my thigh. "You must understand, Candice, that I am not some dumb mutt who refuses to look beyond their stubborn beliefs," Kyril informs, voice stern as I stand up from my chair, watching as the King grabs the dress I was just in, holding it out as he sees where some of the fabric is missing. "I see more than what the naked eye can, I can hear things not even spoken aloud, and I can read someone like you within a matter of seconds." I keep my cool, reminding myself to not lash out for he could be going elsewhere with this conversation than an attack. "We are mates, I can feel it, I know that we are meant for one another," he pauses, looking back to me, "but I also know that we cannot be."

"What do you mean?" I ask, hesitant to ask anything more.

Kyril shakes his head, throwing the dress to the floor as he crosses his arms, eyes beginning to darken. "Perhaps in another life we become true lovers and spend our days growing old together, but here, in this life, we are caught in a battle of desires and wants that keep us apart. We are stubborn people, Candice, equals in our own rights, both wanting something from the same man but having different intentions for his use. However, in this life, we have met on a battlefield, weapons drawn, and already knowing we cannot alter our destiny."

"What are you trying to say? What is the objective of this conversation?" My chest rises and falls quickly, scared of what this King could do to me.

"I could never harm you, Candice, never to bring a sword to that neck of yours. I will never hold you within my presence against your will- "

"You bastard," I snap, fists clenched. "You destroyed the mirror for me to return home. You held me with you against my will by destroying my only known way back home and then forced me to go back with you." My body is tense, expecting him to lash out and come at me with his fists formed. "You now say that you would never do anything to harm me or keep me against my will, but are you so blind that you forget what has happened not even a month ago?"

Kyril nods, agreeing with me as I find my anger rising. "When Heka is found, it is fair game, Candice, but I will not kill you. You find him and keep him from my harm, he is yours and I will not hunt him down for I know you are only using him to return home. However, if I find him, Candice, he is mine, and I will deal the justice he has long awaited." Little does Kyril know what is in store for him in just an hour or two. No one must die, but both my father and Kyril have been wanting to kill the other longer than I have been here in Iduna. "Does that sound fair to you?"

"Yes, it does," I find myself agreeing, my throat running dry as I try and think of what is running through the King's head. I want to know is he suspects an attack tonight, but even more, if he found out I was Heka's daughter if he would disregard this whole agreement and want me dead next.

Kyril runs a hand through his hair, letting out a stressful sigh. "You have no perception of the agony this puts me through, Candice," he begins, looking to me with a sense of despair. I have never seen him this way, looking so broken and guilty. "Perhaps it is because you are human that you cannot feel the attraction we have for one another, the instincts to protect the other and want each other close...but I also know it is because we are not meant to be in this life." I hold myself high, hearing these words of sorrow from a man who never likes to show his weakness of emotions. "I wish we had never met on a battlefield, Candice, but in a different setting where you have fallen for me just as I have for you. You may be human, but I see you as an equal, something I have never called another." Kyril takes his leave and I simply watch, the King not even bothering to shut my door as he calls to me from down the hall, telling me that the dinner is ready.

My eyes are locked at the hallway before me, shoulders tensed, a hallow feeling filling my chest as a part of me pleads not to go, to stay here and let fate deal down below. But I know that cannot happen, that I cannot just sit by and watch things unfold without any control. I will not kill anyone tonight, but I know that I cannot just let my father kill someone. I cannot just step aside and act like my father murdering even one person is acceptable and try to be loyal to him. No one has to die tonight, but I know that is an unreal wish to be made. Taking in a deep breath, I close my eyes, trying to relax the best I can as my nerves are like a bomb within me, only more pressure being applied by the second the longer I try and avoid the night ahead.

I step outside the room, following the hallway down as I can feel my heart beating fast in my chest, my head spinning with questions, and my stomach turning into millions of knots. Tonight, I find my father, or I lose him. If I am trapped here with none of his knowledge to find my way back home, I can honestly say I have no idea what I will do. Stepping into the massive dining room, a feast laid out on the long, marble table, Lucretia motions for me to sit beside her at the edge of the table, right next to Kyril. With her at the head of the table and everyone taking their seats, the King turns to me, offering me a soft smile as his eyes shown only pain as he gazes upon me. He truly believes that we are made perfect for one another, yet he is willing to let me go tonight because he does not want to stand in my way another than he already has.

With my hands folded in my lap and Kyril looking at me from the corner of his eye, as everyone else takes to their seats and the chandelier that hangs from above made from the ceiling made from white horns of an animal, my eyes follow the balcony running above the room. I can sense that the balcony above is where my father will be tonight, perhaps holding a bow and arrow like he did years ago when he slayed Kyril's father. The sword strapped to my thigh is cold, the sharp tip poking at my skin as I fear one swift movement will wedge the hilt into my skin. Lucretia rises to her feet, looking to her guests as her dress is white, falling to the floor with a long train, her chest barely covered as the locket hangs low, the dragon scales only on display.

"Fellow guests of the King, companions of his majesty, and weary travelers of Iduna, welcome to the Zella Palace," Lucretia begins, briefly looking to me as she offers me a sly smile. "This evening, tonight, and until you set out for your travel tomorrow, we welcome you with open arms and hope that you may find a haven within these white walls." Kyril shifts in his seat, not keen on Lucretia's welcoming speech as I look across to Duke Gravon, someone who has avoided me since. He fears me for my human status, for what Dregh warned Kyril about, and that he knows Dregh sealed us off from for a private conversation. Duke Gravon is tense, not looking my way as he keeps his eyes locked on Lucretia, lips pressed together in a firm line. "Let us eat."

The food before us looks similar to what I would expect at some family holiday meal, minus the fattening sides. There is sliced meat on a silver platter, circling a bowl of fresh blue and red berries. Salads are the main side, green leaves with a dark white nut, pastel pink berries, and various versions of the salad spread across the table. Water in glass goblets lay before each plate, designs carved into the pristine glass, the whole setup of the meal perfect, just like I would expect it to be, but I know soon it will become a catastrophe. Where everyone is placed, Kyril's most skilled warriors are not seated close to him, but rather at the opposite end of the table next to elves who hold their heads high and do not wish to grant them any sign of respect. Duke Gravon is Kyril's most trusted companion and although he sits across the King, he is not close enough to protect him. Lucretia seated me next to the King because she believes that I will allow my father to kill Kyril, that I will not try and save the King from death. If I saw my father in the balcony above, about to kill Kyril, would I just simply sit and allow it all to take place? If this was all back home, happening to where I was to be placed against my morals, would I just watch someone be murdered and not help?

"How many days will you and your men be out in the mountains?" Lucretia asks Kyril, starting the first form of conversation as I take a bite of the meat. It tastes like salmon, nothing like I would have expected as it also holds a slightly bitter aftertaste. I recall taking a glance to the mountains ahead, the scorched ruins of a castle by frozen falls. "It is winter, brutal weather out there this time of the season." Lucretia knows they are not headed to the mountains for training, no, but for finding Heka.

Kyril finishes chewing the meat, looking to Lucretia as you can tell they are not fond of one another at all. Their stares towards one another indicates perhaps a history of unpleasant tales and betrayal. "Two weeks, we plan to reach the other edge of the mountains where there is a post for the army out there."

A long pause fills the room as no other conversation takes place, everyone waiting to see what Lucretia is to say. "Forgive me, your majesty, but it seems to me that many of your men are more like scholars than future palace guards." Lucretia is beginning to point out the flaws in the King's lie. "Most would think these men to be hunters of knowledge rather then men to protect their ruler." Lucretia is right, for many of these men are scholars, men talented in tracking based off of science or skilled in archeology rather than trained in wielding a weapon. Only a dozen of the men here are actually warriors, armed and ready to protect their King.

"Are you questioning your rule?" Duke Gravon speaks up, coming to the aid of his king. If there is one person I could select who would take a bullet for his King, or in this case, an arrow or the strike of a sword, it would be Duke Gravon. "His majesty had grace to come and seek shelter within this tribe after the treason you committed against the kingdom of Iduna three decades ago." What did Lucretia and her tribe do to Iduna? Kyril's father was still the ruler at the time, Iduna untouched by my father's wicked deeds. "You and your people should have been hung from the gallows for all to see."

"Enough," Lucretia snaps, rising to her feet as her eyes become a dark gray, the silver rings around her pupils almost glowing. "We paid our wrongs and served the time, we learned our lesson."

Duke Gravon rises to his feet, a darkness surrounding him that I have never witnessed before. "Traitors never learn their lessons. Thieves will always be thieves. Murders will never regret the blood on their hands. But most of all, those who try and betray the ruler of Iduna will always be disloyal and seek their revenge."

"My father was a wise man," Kyril informs, coming into the argument as his warriors are on guard to protect their King. "Wise but foolish in who much he believed in the innerworkings of mercy. He thought grace could turn any soul around for the good, but he did not understand that a woman who feeds off the soul of dark creatures can never respect a second chance." Silence floods the hall, Lucretia trying to think of her next response as I catch a shadow from above, one of a cloaked figure.

My father has come for Kyril.

"We cannot escape our innate destiny, we cannot rewrite who we are within," Lucretia snaps, her sharp teeth on display as the green scales around her chest seem to glow, a red light behind aiding to her frightening look. "We are all savages beneath our fancy clothes, articulation of words, and the masks we put on every morning." My eyes stay locked to the balcony above, a tall figure holding out a white bow as my heart skips a beat. "Gods will always be the demons we seek to destroy, werewolves will always be hunters of the weak, elves will always be the ones to see beyond silly customs and beliefs, humans will always be weak and caught up in our world by fate, and demi-gods will always be a threat to the stability of Iduna. We elves are to purify the kingdom that once was Iduna while you demi-gods will always be here to taint it."

The blood pumps through my veins as I realize that no one can hide from fate, no one can run as fast as they can from it. Time seems to run slow, almost lost in existence as I watch my father pull back the onyx arrow, Lucretia still yelling at Kyril, and Kyril unaware of what is to happen. Do I sit by and stay loyal to my father and his twisted morals, or do I stick up for what I believe and take a risk?

As I watch the arrow release from my father's hand, I watch his eyes in the darkness, how they glow bright blue, focused not on his long-forgotten daughter but on his mission.

As the arrow passes over the table and it about to pierce the King's flesh, I grab the King by his shoulder, slamming him forward, head hitting the table as the arrow brushes the top of his hair, landing in the wall opposite of my father. Kyril acts fast, looking up to me with dark eyes, grabbing my arm as he wonders what I have done, but then he sees it, the arrow. Just as he turns to look where the shot came from, another one is show, the arrow piercing through the air as I grab the King again, pulling him behind me as I look to the balcony above, my father vanishing. As I turn to look at Lucretia, I see her eyes wide as she stares to me, chest glowing red like fire as her eyes become hooded. Acting fast, I pull out the dagger she gave me, ready to attack her, but she strikes first, a shockwave hitting me in the chest as I am shot across the room.

Head banging against the wall and my bones in pain, I watch as the High One who destroyed the soul of a god walks towards me, hitting the King with a blue light that knocks him out of her way. The elves and Kyril's men begin to fight, blood already spilt as Dregh said it would. "You will regret ever getting in my way, human," she shouts, raising her hand again as a dark magic is present, the color of blood, the purpose of her shot is to kill me. Acting fast, I get to my feet, in immense pain as I charge to the elf, not caring if she is getting her magic ready to use. I throw the first punch, landing it right at her nose as she stumbles back, her magic lost for a short second as I swing my leg up, hitting her in the stomach as I see Kyril from the corner of my eye, sliding me his sword. As it skids across the floor and Lucretia grabs my elbow, slamming me onto the floor, I grab the handle of the weapon.

As she twists my elbow and I cry out in pain, I swing my body around, leaving her grasp as I acknowledge that it is either her or me that must die today. In one swift movement, I have landed the blade into her side, watching as she screams, falling to her knees as she is on my level now. The two of us on our knees, her white dress drenched in blood and my hand holding the sword to have caused her fall, the scales upon her skin turn black. Her eyes meet mine, looking lifeless as a small smile spreads across her face. "You silly little human," she chokes, coughing up blood at the same time, her body weak and lose to death. "You have no idea what you have just caused to your existence."

A soft beam of sunlight shines upon my face, the sunset taking place as I watch the first person I have ever slayed fall to the ground. Dregh said this would happen, she warned me what would happen.

"Candice, get back from her," Kyril shouts, his tone dead serious as I look to him, his hands covered in blood as an elf lays limp at his feet.

"She's dead, what harm could she do?" I question, dropping my sword as I look to the woman who was said to be powerful beyond belief.

"It is not her you should be worried about," Duke Gravon informs, still holding his weapon as if he is expecting another attack, "but the soul of the dragon still present within her."

My skin runs pale and I stumble back, rising to my feet instantly as I watch a dark magic from within the body of the elf stir. As my back meets the cold wall I was slammed against, a dark mist rises from the body of Lucretia, the dark matter burning like coals on a fire, moving like a cloud as my feet are frozen in place and I fell like I may have a heart attack.

Just as I take a step to the left, to try and reach Kyril whose hands are cupped together, a swarm of golden flakes circling like a tornado, the soul of the dragon moves quickly, following me as its shape takes on a massive dragon, the mist swarming around me as I find myself becoming lightheaded. The dragon's soul roars at me, the sound shaking the walls as its eyes are bright like fire. The moment I try and run, it comes at me, jaws opening wide as its fire consumes me, the bright red flames engulfing my body as I feel no pain, only fear. As gust of wind glows the dragon at me, engulfing my entire body as my lungs burn and my body feels a burning within.

I collapse to my feet, unable to breath as I try and find any source of air, scratching at the floor as tears fall down my face. My nails dig into the marble floor, as if some new strength, taking pieces of marble with me as I look into the eyes of Kyril. But rather than trying to help me, he backs away. They all back away from me, both elf and Kyril's men, afraid of me. I roll onto my back, trying to catch my breath as my hands wrap around my throat, my brain pulsing in my skull as tears just roll down my face. Looking to the floor, to where my tears have fallen, I find myself wanting to scream as my left hand comes to view, scales beneath my skin, faint but present as I wan to vomit.

"What do we do?" Duke Gravon asks, afraid as his eyes look at me with a fear I have never seen before. Looking to Kyril, I watch him, how he examines me, eyes watering as he just shakes his head.

"There is nothing we can do but pray," he responds softly, taking one small step closer to me. "After all, she has consumed the entire soul of a dragon trapped within an elf for decades."

With those words, I gain my first breath of air since the beast consumed me...or I consumed the beast.

Epilogue

Nothing feels the same anymore, my entire body aching, my head spinning, and joints feeling aged sixty years. As I rise to my feet, shivers run down my back as I can feel my heartbeat, but it is slower than every before, as if nonexistent as it barely beats. I blink my eyes rapidity, my vision trying to focus as if I have gained a new prescription, my vision still blurry as my eyes undergo strain to adjust. My joints pop as I roll my shoulder back, trying to regain the strength I had before Lucretia had thrown me against a wall and I found myself consuming the soul of a dragon. As my body is weak, there is a stir within me, one with a strength I have never felt before, as if I feel light on my feet, able to move swiftly, and my back, my back feels muscles flexing that it never had felt before.

Someone calls my name, their voice loud as my ears ring, my hands shooting up to over my ears as the noises around me are beyond loud. I can hear heartbeats other than my own, ones that beat fast, I can even hear the light steps they take upon the ground, their lungs taking in air, and their scent, I can smell every fiber on their body. My eyes begin to adjust to the light as a warm ray of sunlight shines upon my figure, the sunset coming to an end as the sky begins to darken outside. Trying to open my eyes wider, it burns my eyes as they look to the figures beginning to focus, the familiar face of Kyril looking as if under a microscope. I always had good vision, but now, it is as if I see every piece of him, the hairs that are raised on the back of his neck, the light freckles dashed across his cheeks and nose, every detail of his eyes, and every small hole in the fabric of his clothes. Nothing feels normal anymore, nothing feels the same.

"Candice," the voice calls out again, this time my ears adjusting to the volume of the voice as I try and calm myself down. "Candice, can you hear me, are you okay?" I look to the young King, eyes watering as the sun still burns my eyes, as if I am seeing light for the first time. "Tell me you are okay."

I nod, rubbing my temples as I try and calm myself down more, try and make the pain go away. "I think I am okay," I reply, my voice cracking as I look around to see the remaining elves and King's men staring at me, fear in their eyes. Looking to my feet, the body of Lucretia lays limp at my feet, white dress stained in her crimson blood, her eyes lifeless, and she looks weak, as if she never held any power. Killed by a human, by a human who swore to a goddess she would never kill anyone, yet here I am, having killed my first enemy. It was in self-defense, yet a piece of me knows that it was not just self-defense, but something that had to be done.

"Heka is still here, your majesty," Duke Gravon interrupts, calling Kyril's attention as I stumble back against the wall, feeling a sudden rush of energy spread across my body. "We must find him and complete the task at hand."

Kyril nods, agreeing with Duke Gravon as he turns to me. "Do not leave this room, Candice, for we will be back soon." I shake my head, knowing that Kyril made that bet with me just an hour ago, that agreement that whoever found him first would get their way with Heka.

"No," I croak, "you said whoever finds him keeps him, that we leave the other alone with Heka, I am going to find him and without your aid. This is where we split on this battlefield, we agree that separating is for our own good now to find our common goal."

Before Kyril can even retort, I leave, moving faster than I ever have before as one second I am in the dining room and the next I find myself down one of the halls. Taking in a deep breath, I try and find any unfamiliar scent, knowing that my father will smell neither werewolf nor elf. He will have a distinct smell that I now will be able to pinpoint. I raise my head high, taking in another deep breath as I close my eyes, focusing on the gust of wind that flows past me, feeling the ground beneath me, the walls around me, the warmth within my soul, and the prescience of someone I felt only minutes ago. My eyes snap open, head turning to the balcony where Lucretia had me hours ago, telling me about both my father and great ancestor who motivated her to consume a soul.

Moving towards the balcony, I spot a figure not draped in black, but a navy cloak, their face hidden by the hood, presence haunting, and their back turned towards me. I walk softly, my nerves picking up as I reach the balcony, the cold winter breezes sending chills down my spine as a warmth from within me replaces the cold. My chest rises and falls with every deep breath I take, my eyes widening as I reach out to the figure, fingers barely brushing the shoulders of the male before he pulls away, spinning around for those piercing blue eyes to meet mine.

"You are not your mother," he says, those words feeling like swords to my heart, his tone harsh, eyes scanning me over. "It was never part of the plan for you to come into this world. Why have you not left it?"

I am shocked that my father, after years of not seeing his only child, would rather greet me with harsh words than ones of welcoming and warmth. "No, I am not my mother, but you should try and at least act like the father you are to me, your daughter, the one you left alone years ago."

"Why did you come here?" he asks, his hands pulling down his hood as the face of my father greets me. What I was used to seeing in old family photos and the tabloids, the face is now before me, the dark locks of hair grown down to his shoulders, more of an aged face, strong jaw, and a scar running along the left side of his face, it all seems so unfamiliar.

"I came to find the man who never once returned home to his family though he had every chance," I respond, taking his words as insults and the message that he does not want me here. "Eleven years, have you no idea the stress and loneliness that put on mom?"

My father shakes his head. "She knew what my mission meant for her, and she accepted my calling. She accepted the fact that I would not return home until my mission was finished."

"Your mission to murder innocent children," I add, voice sharp as my father tilts his head to the side.

"You do not understand, Candice, but those children, those things, are not pure, are not normal, and must die. For centuries our family has sworn to hunt down the gods and their children, to keep the world of the supernatural more mortal that immortal. Those gods and their children, they are nearly threats to our reality back home."

I step back, understanding why I now wanted to find my father. "You have no right to call the human realm your home, for you have lost that privilege," I spit, feeling a darkness stirring within me. I know why I still wanted to find my father after I accepted the fact that he would never come back home. I was so foolish, so blind. "You are not deserving of mom either."

"Then why did you come here, Candice, to Iduna, to me?" Heka shouts, raising his hands in the air as my eyebrows knit together.

"Because I thought having you back not just in my life, but mom's as well, that we could be a family again, that our lives could be happy once more," I snap, shaking my head as my eyes water, "but now I do not know who you are, and I am too deep into this game of Dregh's now to back down."

"Dregh?" he asks, concerned. "You met Dregh?"

There is a noise down the hall, the scent of Kyril growing closer. "We have no idea, Kyril and his men are coming for you and I need you alive so I can get out of here."

"What did Dregh want from you?" Heka asks again, making sure I get the message that he will not move unless I tell him.

Looking over my shoulder, I spot Kyril, his eyes locked with mine as he sees I have beaten him to Heka. My arm is grabbed, pulling me back to the focus of my father as he asks his question again. "Because she wants me for a sick game of hers, to take down the gods because you are not strong enough to. Now, we must leave." Heka looks past me and to Kyril, his eyes turning back as he whispers words to himself, a dark energy circling his hands as he pushes past me. "No, come back."

Heka walks into the hallway, ignoring my calls. I rush after my father, seeing him raising his fists to Kyril who instructs his men to ready their weapons. "We had a deal, Kyril, do not harm him," I shout at the King, his golden eyes focused on my father. "You made me a deal, you said you would never do anything to harm your mate and by doing this, you will have harmed me."

My father stops, lowering his hands as his magic dissipates. All eyes are on me, even Kyril's golden eyes that remind me of a summer sunset. "This monster is your mate?" Heka asks me, voice sharp as I know what my words mean to him, how to be mates with someone he has sword to kill must betray him. "You, a descendent of Heka of the Nile and my daughter, mated to the very creature our family has sword to destroy?"

"Leave him alone, father, and come with me, leave this one be, have mercy on this one demi-god because your daughter pleads with you to."

Silence, the tension of the air growing in power as Kyril looks at me now not with any emotion of attraction or admiration, but with despair and disbelief. Just as I think my father is to agree to my terms, he places his focus on Kyril, landing a blow right at the King, only for Kyril to block it with a forcefield of bright red flames. "You bastard," Heka shouts at Kyril, grabbing a dagger form his belt as he lunges it at Kyril, only, as I think of nothing else that can be done, I thrust myself into the battle, blocking the hit from my father with my arms crossed on each other. As the dagger meets my locked wrists, the blade shatters against my flesh, a set of gray scales covering my wrists to protect the blow. The force of my shield thrusts my father back a few yards, giving me time to look back to Kyril, despair reflected in his eyes.

"You were the daughter of the man I swore to kill this whole time," Kyril whispers in disbelief. "My mate the daughter of my sworn enemy, what dark humor must the gods have to craft such a curse."

I shake my head. "Respect the treaty we made, that I am to go off with Heka on my own terms because I have found him first. Respect me because we are equals like you said, because you could never do harm to me."

"Yet you have harmed me more than anyone ever has," Kyril whispers, voice weak, "and you use that to get what you want, because you know how much you mean to me."

I do not reply, simple watching as the King's eyes water, trying to hold his strong and powerful character to prove to his men the masculinity they believe him to have. "Let me have my father, Kyril, let us keep our agreement with no betrayal," I plead, keeping my voice soft, my tone more nurturing than anything as I try and keep the king calm.

The world around us is tuned out, our eyes focused on the other, the dragon within me only beginning to awaken. "You are the slyest fox I have ever met, Candice, and do you know what pains me the most?" Kyril asks, hand reaching upon, his fingers brushing across my cheek, as if trying to memorize the feeling of my skin, his hands pulling my face close to his.

"That you must let me go?" I ask, guessing the answer to his question, watching as his eyes scan every feature of my face.

A finger brushes across my bottom lip, Kyril pulling away as he hesitates to et me go. "The fact that you are the first person in my life that makes me feel alive, like I have experienced the beauty of life, and that makes this miserable world so much better, yet I must let you go."

Kyril pulls away, taking a step back as he looks back to Heka. "Go, the two of you, just leave." Nodding my head, I back away, keeping my eyes fixed on the King who has sacrificed his sole mission all because of a human who wanted to find her father. A human who he had no control over falling for. "And Candice," he calls out, calling my attention back to him once again. "The next time we see one another, I fear you may not even recognize the person you have become."

A hand is placed upon my shoulder, my father pulling me away from the King. Both men have decided to put their goals aside all because of me, because of something they care for. My father will be here for me, to help me, to guide me through this new life of a dragon within me, and Kyril...he will wait till he can see me again. With every step I take, my body feels weaker rather than stronger like what I would have thought. As my father guides me out of the palace and we keep our words the bare minimum, my vision begins to blur once more, my feet beginning to drop over small bricks in the passage to the mountains. The cold air consumes my weak body, my father whispering spells to keep us warm.

I cough, covering it with my elbow as my body feels weaker instantly. Pulling my arm down, I look to where I coughed, my skin paling as I see the crimson substance staining my sleeve. "Father," I call out, my father stopping in his steps a few meters away. As he looks back to me, he sees the blood, but it is not the blood that scares him, but something else wrong with me.

"Candice, your...your hands," he whispers in disbelief as his eyes are focused on my flesh. My eyes quickly snap to my hands, to what used to be fair skin is now a set of hands, the veins running through almost glowing, the blue veins creating patterns within my skin as I fall to my knees. My fingertips are stained a midnight blue, my wrists covered in dark scales, and as I frantically pull my sleeves up to reveal my arms holding the same blue vein pattern, I look in horror to Heka.

"No," I mutter, shaking my head. "No." I look to my chest, pulling the top down to where I can get a clear view of where my heart pumps, dark blue scales running from my chest and fading away as they reach my collarbones. There, in my chest, where my heart is, beats my black heart, each pump visible just like on Dregh's own chest, the sight making me want to vomit. "Make it go away, make it go away, Heka, make it go away" I scream, tears running down my face I as frantically scrape at my chest, hoping the scales will peal away and be gone. As my fingernails begin to dig into my flesh and rather than the scales coming off, blood begins to trickle down my chest, I look up to my father, hopelessness flooding my entire existence as he looks at me with worry. "No."

Pain rises from within me, my screams filling the air as I fling my arms out, a power surge running through my body, and as my hands clench into fists and those beautiful eyes that hold every galaxy run through my mind, I lower my fists. As they hit the ground, a black smoke explodes around me, running out like a shockwave as Heka cowers from the magic I have just released into the world. His face is pale, eyes hollow as he looks at me like he does not even know who I am anymore.

"What am I?" I cry out, unable to accept the answer that awaits. I do not want to accept the answer that awaits, I do not want to hear it, but I know I must.

Heka shakes his head, looking at me with fear in his eyes. "You are no longer a human, Candice," he begins, my heart plummeting to the ground as I want to run away, "you are something more powerful than what I have ever seen."

"And what is that?" I ask, wanting to give up and fall asleep on the forest floor, to perhaps wake up back in my bed and greet my mother with a warm smile. "What am I, father?"

"I do not know."

www.ingramcontent.com/pod-product-compliance
Lightning Source LLC
Chambersburg PA
CBHW070946190726
48292CB00004B/1355